**LUCY TURNED THE KEY AND
OPENED THE DOOR TO HER CABIN—
ONLY TO DISCOVER A GUY
LOUNGING ON ONE OF THE BEDS!**

Then she realized it wasn't just any guy.
She was standing a few feet away from the
soccer player she'd seen earlier on the field.

The guy stood up, confused. "This
must be a mistake, right?"

Lucy laughed and nodded. "Unless
your name is Sabrina, then yes, this is a
mistake."

The guy grinned. "I could be Sabrina,
sure." He held up his roommate assignment. "And my roommate's named
Robin—that could be a guy or a girl. Is
your name Robin?" he asked hopefully.

Lucy laughed again. *This guy, whoever
he is, is charming.*

DON'T MISS THESE

7th Heaven.

BOOKS!

NOBODY'S PERFECT
MATT'S STORY
MARY'S STORY
MIDDLE SISTER
MR. NICE GUY
THE PERFECT PLAN
RIVALS
SECRETS
THE NEW ME
SISTER TROUBLE
LEARNING THE ROPES
DRIVE YOU CRAZY
CAMP CAMDEN

AND COMING SOON

LUCY'S ANGEL
WINTER BALL

7th Heaven™

CAMP CAMDEN

by Amanda Christie

An Original Novel

*Based on the hit TV series
created by Brenda Hampton*

Random House 🏠 New York

Published in the United States by
Random House, Inc., New York,
and simultaneously in Canada
by Random House of Canada Limited, Toronto.

www.randomhouse.com/kids

Library of Congress Control Number: 2001086306
ISBN: 0-375-81360-8

Printed in the United States of America
First Edition
July 2001
10 9 8 7 6 5 4 3 2 1

RANDOM HOUSE and colophon are
registered trademarks of Random House, Inc.

7th Heaven™

CAMP CAMDEN

ONE

It was early Saturday morning at the Camdens', and already the house was bustling with activity.

Lucy Camden stuffed several CDs into her suitcase, then looked at her watch for what was certainly the five hundredth time.

Eight-fifty. In ten minutes, she and her little sister, Ruthie, were leaving for a weeklong summer camp in sunny Malibu, California.

This was Lucy's last real break before starting college—and she intended to enjoy every minute of it!

"I'm taking Dad's guitar," a little voice proclaimed. Lucy turned around and saw

Ruthie coming up the attic steps, clutching all the goodies she wanted to take to camp.

She looks like an overdecorated Christmas tree, Lucy thought, trying not to laugh. Bulging, colorful bags hung from Ruthie's hands and shoulders like heavy ornaments. A mini golf club dangled from her belt. Art supplies and candy stashes spilled out of her pockets.

"How do you plan to carry a guitar when you don't have room for your toothbrush?" Lucy asked.

Ruthie shrugged. *"You* can carry it."

Lucy's eyebrow went up. "In case you've forgotten, there's a *one bag* per camper rule. You need to take what's essential and leave the rest at home. And you need to hurry."

Ruthie sighed and headed back down to her room, dropping a line of chocolate malt balls behind her. Suddenly, Happy sprang down the second-floor hallway from Reverend and Mrs. Camden's bedroom, overjoyed at her good luck. But before the dog could lap up the chocolate balls, Mrs. Camden walked out, reached down, and grabbed the remaining candies.

"Ruthie! You know these make Happy sick!"

But Ruthie had already disappeared into her bedroom. Mrs. Camden sighed and started up the stairs to the attic. She poked her head into Lucy's room.

Lucy glared at her mother. "Don't distract her," Lucy pleaded. "She's finally narrowed herself down to three bags, and we have"—Lucy glanced at her watch—"seven minutes to get rid of two more."

Mrs. Camden walked inside. "I can't believe it," she said, surveying the room. "A year ago, my two oldest daughters shared this room. Now, in a few short weeks, it'll be empty."

Lucy shook her head. "No, it won't. In a few short weeks, Simon and Ruthie will be fighting for it."

"My point is that you and Mary will both be gone."

The memory of Mary often saddened Mrs. Camden. Less than a year ago, she and her husband had made the hardest decision of their lives, sending the troubled young woman off to live with her grandfather. Now Mary was all the way across the country in Buffalo, New York. Although Mary's strict grandfather had been a good influence on her, she rarely came to visit.

Lucy hugged her mother. "And Mary and I will both be back for visits. So no worries, Mom, okay? Especially when there are still four other kids in the house."

Just then, Simon emerged from the stairs. "Aren't you gone yet?" he asked Lucy.

Lucy picked up her CD boom box. "Why are you in such a hurry?"

"No reason," Simon quipped, and disappeared as quickly as he had come.

Moments later, Lucy stuck her head in Ruthie's bedroom. The place looked like a tornado had ripped through it. Every imaginable household item—especially those with the potential for creating fun or mischief—was strewn across the room. Play-Doh, dishwashing liquid, rubber bands . . .

"Ruthie?" Lucy called.

A curly brown head emerged from the closet. "I'm ready," Ruthie declared. She had a suitcase in one hand, and a fishing pole in the other.

Lucy shook her head. "If you can't fit the fishing pole in the suitcase, the camp sponsors will take it from you. There's a space requirement on the bus."

"But you're taking a boom box."

Lucy nodded. "Yes, but I'm a camp teacher."

Ruthie clasped the fishing pole tighter and stepped over the mounds of kid junk. "Yeah, but I'm on scholarship," she argued. "I'm special."

Reverend Camden, who had just appeared in the doorway, cocked his head as Ruthie marched out of her room with both her bag and fishing pole in tow. He looked at Lucy and shrugged. "She *is* special. Sometimes a little *too* special."

Lucy laughed and gave her father a kiss on the cheek. "Thanks for letting us go, Dad."

The reverend's pride was apparent in the smile on his face. "Don't thank me. You're the one who was invited by the camp board to teach the carpentry class. You earned it, Luce."

Suddenly, her mother called from downstairs. "Get moving, girls! You two don't want to miss the bus, do you?"

* * *

Ten minutes later, Lucy and Ruthie hauled their luggage toward the check-in line at the bus station. Against Lucy's advice, Ruthie held her fishing pole out defiantly, hoping that her confidence would serve as a shield against any meddlesome adults.

Just then, a short, square woman with broad shoulders motioned Lucy and Ruthie over to her check-in table. She wore a badge that said MRS. STOUT, and looked like an army sergeant.

"Names?" she demanded.

Lucy smiled and pointed to her name on the list. "Camden. Lucy Camden. And this is Ruthie."

Mrs. Stout didn't look up. "Ruthie *what*?"

Lucy politely replied, "Camden."

The woman checked both names off her list, then glanced at Lucy's boom box. "I have to confiscate that. You're going to an outdoor camp, not a street party."

Lucy nodded respectfully. "I'm sorry, I forgot to explain. I'm not a camper; I'm the carpentry teacher."

Mrs. Stout shook her head. Clearly,

that didn't matter to the woman.

Lucy continued. "According to the rules and regulations, teachers are allowed a second bag or size-equivalent item. And since there was no rule barring stereos—"

Mrs. Stout sized up Lucy. "This is *my* rule, not the camp's rule. Campers don't appreciate rap music at four in the morning. And neither do *I*."

Rap music? Lucy would have laughed out loud if she wasn't trying so hard to be diplomatic. She smiled again. "I understand the complications of communal living. If all the campers don't respect one another's rights, then nobody has a good time. Which is why I intend to use my stereo with the utmost courtesy."

Mrs. Stout coolly replied, "You won't be using it at all. And you should learn right now that you can't lawyer your way out of trouble."

Frustrated, Lucy handed Mrs. Stout the boom box—as a delighted Ruthie snickered and sneaked right by with her fishing pole.

Back at the Camden house, Simon was already scoping out Lucy's room. He had big plans for the week. And if those plans succeeded, he might even be able to extend them well into his high school years.

A voice from the hall shook him from his thoughts. "I'm here while the girls are gone."

He turned and found his big brother, Matt, who enjoyed visiting home during his college downtime. Matt stepped into Lucy's room, looked in her mirror, and flexed his bicep muscles. "The guys rule the roost now," he said to Simon. "You, me, Dad, and the twins—Samuel and David . . ."

But Simon was uninterested and waved his big brother's thoughts away. "I don't have time for male bonding, Matt. I have to get my office in order."

Matt looked at him and laughed. "Office?"

Simon pulled out his new cell phone and punched in several numbers. "Lucy's room is more conducive to my needs than Ruthie's."

"And what *needs* might those be?"

A small screen popped up on Simon's cell phone. Inside the frame was a list of items, which Simon read off. "Phone line next to the electrical sockets, power strip, plenty of desk space, and proper overhead lighting."

The industrious ninth grader looked up at his big brother just long enough to offer an apologetic shrug. "Summer isn't about fun and games for me, Matt. I've decided to invest in the stock market."

TWO

Lucy pulled her bag out from under her bus seat and retrieved her camp brochure and notes. Even though she had read the glossy brochure several times, she thought that a little brushup on the coming week couldn't hurt. Not only that, she was excited. Reading the pages again made the two-hour trip to camp more bearable.

Inside the brochure was a personal letter from the camp board. Lucy unfolded it and read the words again. In it, the board explained that they had heard about the work she had done as a volunteer for Habitat for Humanity—a group that helped build homes for poor families in critical need of housing.

Little did she know that that work would land her a one-week guest position teaching at one of the best summer camps in California. Now she would teach the carpentry skills she had learned to kids and teenagers who had an interest in construction.

Although it wasn't an official part of her job description, Lucy also planned to try and recruit kids for Habitat for Humanity.

Lucy flipped open her notebook and glanced over the first page, which contained the outline for her class. Because a week wasn't long enough for a group of new students to build a house, she had decided to teach them how to build a clubhouse. First they would draw up a blueprint, and then they would follow the plans through from beginning to end. Once the clubhouse was complete, they would dedicate it to the camp, which could use it any way it saw fit.

Lucy began scribbling down new thoughts, energized by the fact that she, a recent high school graduate, was being allowed to *teach*! It was almost too good to be true. Maybe she would discover that she was good at it, and take education as her minor while in college.

Suddenly, a friendly girl plopped down next to her and extended her hand to shake. A tiny set of oars was stitched across the upper right side of her shirt.

"Tara Klein," she announced, noticing Lucy's notebook. "I'm a teacher, too. Rowing."

Lucy shook the girl's hand. "Wow, how did you get into rowing?"

The girl grinned. "It's a family thing. I grew up in Minnesota, on the lakes. What about you? What are you teaching?"

Lucy smiled, knowing the response that her answer would elicit. "I'm the carpentry teacher."

Tara's vibrant face suddenly looked perplexed. "*Carpentry?* You mean you build things with saws and hammers and stuff?"

Lucy nodded. "Yep."

Tara laughed. "Wow. I was expecting you to say cheerleading or something. Carpentry—that's kind of cool."

Suddenly, Tara's eyes caught something on Lucy's letter. She frowned. "Uh-oh," she said.

"What?" Lucy asked.

Tara pointed to a line that read: *Your cabin roommate will be Sabrina Van Raming.*

Tara's face was getting more contorted by the second.

"Do you know her?" Lucy asked.

Tara leaned over and whispered. "You see that girl in the very last seat?"

Lucy turned around. There were two girls sitting together. "Which one?"

Tara laughed. "Which one could turn you to ice?"

Lucy looked again, trying to appear nonchalant. One girl was plump, plain, and quiet. The other one looked like she just stepped off a high-fashion New York runway. She was wearing shiny red pants that hung low across her hips, and her sequined tube top was as retro-hip as they come. Her legs were crossed, with a glossy magazine spread across them, and her daintily painted toenails peeked out from a funky pair of high-heeled sandals.

Everything about her was intimidating, Lucy noted with a slight twinge of jealousy. She held a gold cell phone in her left hand,

and chatted to some unknown person while turning her back to the practically invisible girl next to her. On anybody else, the look would have been excessive and overly exposed. But on this girl, it was sheer glamour.

Lucy looked back at Tara, who raised an annoyed eyebrow. "Need I say more?"

"*That's* my roommate?" Lucy wearily asked. As much as she hated the idea of competing with other girls, it was hard not to feel inferior when compared to someone so ultratrendy.

Tara nodded. "All the girls call her Miss Priss because she thinks she's so high and mighty. She won't lower herself to talk to anybody. Not even the guys—who follow her around like puppy dogs. It's so sick."

"Where does she get those clothes?" Lucy asked, trying hard to hide her envy. They were so unique, so *expensive*.

"Where do you think? She teaches the modeling class. You see that magazine? She's probably looking at pictures of *herself*."

Lucy couldn't mask her shock. "You mean she's an actual working fashion model?"

Tara rolled her eyes. "And she knows it."

Two seats behind Lucy, Ruthie was glad to be sitting alone. She was determined to have her own identity at camp, and hoped Lucy would give her some breathing room. After all, she wasn't a fourth grader anymore. She was moving up in the world— she was a *tweenager*. And having a big sister at camp wasn't exactly cool.

Suddenly, Ruthie felt a yank on her curls. She shot up in her seat and looked around. In the seat behind her, a blond boy dropped out of sight.

She leaned over the seat back and glared at him. He threw up his hands in mock innocence. "I didn't do it!"

He's cute, Ruthie noted. She stuck out her tongue and dropped back into her seat.

Meanwhile, at home in Glenoak, Simon was already busy at work. He had just finished setting up a laptop computer. One by one, the curious Camdens were dropping by Lucy's room.

Mrs. Camden appeared in the doorway first. She cracked a smile. "Matt said you're trading stocks on the Internet?"

Simon nodded and climbed underneath the desk. He began inspecting the phone jack. "Could we get the phone company out here to install a DSL line?"

"A what?" Mrs. Camden asked.

"So my computer will be faster."

The silence that followed prompted Simon to stick his head out from under the desk. Mrs. Camden had her hands on her hips. She was not amused by his request.

Simon climbed back out, defending himself. "Things change so quickly on Wall Street—a twenty-second delay could put me out of business."

Mrs. Camden's hands didn't move from her hips. "Where did you get that computer?"

Simon smiled. "From my after-school investment club."

"But school's out for the summer."

"I liked the club so much, I agreed to help mentor new students in a summer program. So to show his appreciation, the sponsor loaned me his old computer. Pretty phat, huh?"

"Pretty *what*?" Mrs. Camden asked.

"Phat," Simon said. "You know—money."

"Money?"

"Cool."

Mrs. Camden nodded, unimpressed. She had lived through the trendy vocabularies of three teenagers already. The word *phat* would be out faster than Ruthie's new Razor scooter had become in. "And how do you intend to pay for this DSL line?"

Simon's smile grew even bigger. "With my high-yield bonds."

Mrs. Camden's curiosity was growing by the second. "How did you afford bonds?"

Simon punched several keys on his computer. A financial graph popped up. He pointed to a sliver of a financial pie chart. "The school club has a fund, and each member is given a portion to invest in a club-monitored account. In addition to that money, I added my baby-sitting funds. See that fat sliver? That's my account. I've made a hefty profit."

Mrs. Camden looked at her fourteen-year-old son. She didn't know whether to be envious or proud. Then she smiled. Of course she was proud.

Simon closed the door and lowered his voice. "You left your bank statement on the kitchen table last week, Mom. I took a look at it." He shook his head sadly. "If you'd like me to manage your money, I'm happy to waive the brokerage fee."

THREE

Finally, the bus turned up a winding dirt road. Tara pointed out the window where rolling green hills were punctuated by rocky crags and long, dense stretches of forest. "On the other side of that hill is the ocean."

Lucy couldn't believe it. The brochure hadn't said anything about the ocean. "Do we get to go to the beach?" she asked.

Tara shook her head. "Only if you sneak out. And Mrs. Stout is always on the lookout."

Lucy's brow furrowed. "Why would they have a beach if we can't use it?"

"Unless you want to dive off a cliff to get down there, you have to brave the trail.

It's pretty steep. Not safe for the younger kids."

The bus turned down a second dirt road, and a few kids pushed down their windows and stuck their heads out.

Ruthie saw the Camp Malibu sign up ahead and let out a cheer. Lucy stuck her head out and saw what Ruthie was cheering about.

Beyond the sign, the camp was far off in the distance, sitting on a crest, with its back to the Pacific Ocean. To the east, rows and rows of horse stables lined the edge of the woods, and a large central cabin was perched on the edge of a lake. Beside the lake was the quad—a giant field of grass, perfect for sporting events.

Tara leaned out the window with Lucy. "See that field? That's where we have the Welcoming Games."

Lucy nodded. "What are they exactly?"

"All the teen coaches gather everyone together, divide them up into teams, and lead the teams in all kinds of sporting competitions. It's a blast."

Lucy had to admit she wasn't looking forward to the games. Sports weren't her favorite pastime. She'd rather build a house or fix a car.

Tara read the look on Lucy's face and smiled. "If you don't like sports, you should volunteer to monitor the games. Then all you have to do is watch."

Lucy grinned at her new friend. "You're the best!"

Minutes later, Lucy ambled off the bus with her suitcase in tow. She had to sign in at the teachers' table, then get the keys to her cabin.

The parking lot was bustling with activity. Kids were shouting each other's names with glee and hugging. Apparently, most of the kids at Camp Malibu had been here before.

A soccer ball whizzed by and the most gorgeous guy Lucy had ever seen raced after it. He was built like all the soccer players at Kennedy High: stocky, muscular, and agile. And from the golden hue of his skin, it was clear that he spent hours on the field beneath the California sun. Sweat dripped from his black hair. He caught up with the ball, stopped it briskly with his toe, whisked it back behind him, spun around, and kicked. The ball immediately arced, flying over the heads of dozens of kids. On the other side of the field, the ball hit its target perfectly: an empty soccer goal.

The guy let out a whoop, and his green eyes brushed past Lucy. *Wow,* Lucy thought, but kept walking.

She found her check-in line and was pleased to see that no one was in it. She walked right up to the table and introduced herself to the man behind it.

"Lucy Camden?" he said. "I know that name. I'm on the board of directors that invited you here. My name's Mr. Sanchez, and we're pleased to have you with us."

Lucy returned his graciousness. "Thank you. I really appreciate the opportunity."

Just then, Lucy heard a voice behind her that she recognized. She turned around and saw Mrs. Stout arguing with somebody. *Typical,* thought Lucy. *If people would just be as nice as Mr. Sanchez, then the world would be a much better place.*

Mr. Sanchez handed Lucy her key and pointed toward a trail leading up into the wooded hills. "Follow that trail, and when it forks, take a right. You'll see Cabin 22 up ahead. Watch out for wildlife."

Lucy thanked the man and picked up her bag. She turned around and suddenly realized who Mrs. Stout was arguing with: Sabrina Van Raming.

Lucy shivered at the thought of fighting with either of them. Then she shoved her negative ideas aside. She was determined to make her roommate situation work, regardless of how disagreeable Sabrina proved to be.

She hoisted her heavy bag over her shoulder, preparing for the long hike to her cabin. Then she remembered why her bag was so heavy. In addition to her basic carpentry tools, she had packed at least twenty CDs—and now she couldn't listen to any of them.

She sighed and headed toward the trail. *Positive thoughts,* she said to herself. *If I think positive thoughts about Sabrina and Mrs. Stout, then everything will work out.*

When she reached the middle of the trail, she suddenly stopped. *Wait a minute . . .*

She turned back around and looked across the field. *Uh-oh.*

She scanned the faces of the countless kids, who from so far away were indistinguishable. Where had Ruthie gone?

Fishing pole in hand, Ruthie walked onto the dock of the lake. She was delighted that everyone else had been distracted by check-in. Now she had the entire lake to herself.

She dropped her suitcase and popped open the clasps. She opened the case and smiled. Inside sat a large jar of live worms, which she had dug out of her mother's garden the night before.

Ruthie grabbed the jar and twisted open the lid. She stuck her nose down inside and smelled. *Mmmm!*

She grabbed the mucky head of the first worm she could wrap her grubby fingers around and started pulling. Or was it the tail she grabbed? The worm stretched and stretched, then finally came loose.

Ruthie held it up and watched it squirm. She wasn't afraid of worms and didn't like people who were. Worms were cool. You could cut them in half and they'd regenerate. Not only that, worms kept soil fresh, and fresh soil helped plants grow. *What could be better than a worm?*

Ruthie pulled up the end of her fishing pole and carefully took the hook in hand. She looked at the worm. "Sorry, pal."

She pushed the hook quickly into the center of its long body. Then she looked out across the lake, searching for the darkest water—where the lake would be the deepest.

She spotted a black circle of water far off to her right. She raised her pole behind her shoulder, then cast as far as she could, lifting her thumb off the line so the reel could spin, just like Grandpa Charles had taught her.

Because the hook was weighted and heavy, she hit the spot perfectly and the line began to sink. A round red bob floated up her line and sat on the surface of the water. Now all Ruthie had to do was watch the bob. If it moved, then a fish had bitten and pulled the line down.

Ruthie leaned back, using her suitcase as a pillow. *This is the life,* she thought to herself, staring up at the sky.

"Better watch that bob," a familiar voice said.

Ruthie looked back and saw Lucy standing behind her. "I am."

Lucy smiled. "I know you're excited to fish, but you need to go to your cabin. I checked in for you, but your counselor is going to worry that you're missing."

Ruthie groaned. "Are you going to act like Mom all week?"

Lucy bent down and kissed the top of her sister's head. "Yes—which means that so long as you act responsibly, I'm going to trust you to behave. Believe it or not, I want a vacation from our family as much as you do. So fish for a few minutes, and then go to Cabin 8—okay?"

Ruthie nodded as Lucy turned to go. Suddenly, she felt a tug on her line. . . .

FOUR

Lucy came to the fork in the trail and turned right. Up ahead, she saw several little cabins, each one tucked away in its own private nook. She sat her bag down for a moment and noted that her surroundings were right out of a storybook. They were serene and beautiful.

Suddenly, a flash of brown caught her eye. She turned and looked into the forest, where she was certain she had seen something trot by.

Then she spotted it. Not fifteen feet away, a baby deer stood staring at her. Lucy held her breath for fear of scaring the creature away.

The two watched one another for what seemed like several minutes, and Lucy was transfixed. Then a doe, the fawn's mother, strolled out of the brush and nudged the little deer away.

Lucy finally let out her breath. *That was intense,* she thought. She quietly picked her bag up and walked toward the cabins.

When Lucy reached Cabin 22, the awe she had just experienced was replaced by a surge of excitement. *I've got my own place, away from Mom and Dad, for one whole week!*

She retrieved her cabin key from her pocket and slid it into the lock. *I hope Sabrina's not here yet. Just the thought of that girl makes me nervous.*

Lucy turned the key and opened the door—only to discover that a dark-haired guy was lounging on one of the beds! Then she realized it wasn't just any guy. She was standing a few feet away from the soccer player she'd seen earlier on the field.

The guy stood up, confused. His clear green eyes were a startling contrast to his black hair. He grinned, and two mischievous dimples appeared in his cheeks. His smile was deadly. "This must be a mistake, right?" he asked.

Lucy laughed and nodded. "Unless your name is Sabrina, then yes, this is a mistake."

The guy grinned. "I could be Sabrina, sure." He held up his roommate assignment. "And my roommate's named Robin—that could be a guy or a girl. Is your name Robin?" he asked hopefully.

Lucy laughed again. *This guy, whoever he is, is charming.* She extended her hand. "Unfortunately, I'm Lucy."

He sighed as he shook her hand. "Well, if you're going to ruin all the fun, then I guess I'm Dirk. Dirk Porter." Then he bowed. "At your service. Get it? Porter? I'm a porter, like at a hotel. Do let me get your bag, miss."

Before Lucy could stop him, he'd hoisted her bag onto the bed, but not without letting out a groan. *"What is in your bag?"*

Lucy grinned. "CDs."

Dirk shook his head. "There's more than CDs in that bag."

"And tools," Lucy confessed.

"Tools?" Dirk asked flatly. "As in metal

tools? As in working-on-a-car tools?"

Lucy nodded. She loved the reaction she always got when talking about her tools. "As in building-a-house tools," she clarified. "I'm the carpentry teacher."

Dirk smiled and crossed his arms. He was clearly impressed.

Just then, the front door opened and Sabrina walked in. Standing in the light of the doorway, her long golden hair shining, she looked even more stunning than before.

To Lucy's surprise, Sabrina held Lucy's confiscated CD boom box in hand. Without introducing herself, or even looking in Lucy's direction, she said, "Here's your stereo."

Sabrina laid it on a table beside Lucy, but before Lucy could thank her, Sabrina turned away. Then she glanced at Dirk coolly, her eyes brushing quickly by him. "Hello, Dirk." Clearly, these two knew one another from previous camps.

Dirk's tan face turned slightly red as he smiled at her. "Hi, Sabrina. So you're the mysterious roommate?"

Sabrina shrugged and tossed her fuzzy

pink bag on the empty bed. "Yeah, I'm so mysterious."

Lucy watched Dirk, who was watching Sabrina dig through her bag. He looked nervous, like he wasn't sure what to say next. Lucy felt her heart sink. *Of course he's nervous. He likes her. What guy wouldn't?*

"We just had a roommate mix-up," Dirk explained. But Sabrina seemed more interested in her compact mirror than she was in him.

He looked at Lucy and reached for his own bag. "Well," he said, searching for words that had suddenly deserted him, "I better go find my cabin. I'll see you two later."

He smiled abruptly, then disappeared out the front door.

Lucy stared at the empty doorway in confusion. *How did things get so awkward so quickly?* She took a determined step toward Sabrina, her anxiety rising.

"Thanks for the stereo."

Sabrina, who now had a pair of tweezers in her hand, was standing near the window, where light illuminated her delicate features. She nodded as she looked in the mirror and plucked a tiny eyebrow hair. But she said nothing.

Lucy bit her lip nervously, unsure of how to break the strange silence that Sabrina had ushered into the room.

"I guess you figured out that I'm Lucy?"

Suddenly, there was the sound of music—the ringing electronic notes of a popular song. It was a cell phone ringing.

Sabrina reached into her bag and pulled out the gold phone Lucy had seen earlier. She quickly tapped a button and held it to her ear.

"Yes?" Sabrina said with a frustrated edge to her voice. She turned her back to Lucy and walked to the corner of the room. Her voice became quieter, almost like a whisper.

At that moment, Lucy felt how she imagined the plain, plump girl on the bus must have felt. Practically nonexistent.

Lucy looked at the stereo, confused by her roommate's contradictory behavior. Clearly, Sabrina wanted to help Lucy by bringing her the boom box—

Then Lucy recalled the fight she had

witnessed earlier when Sabrina had gone head to head with Mrs. Stout. Had that fight been about Lucy's stereo? But if so, why was Sabrina so chilly now?

Ruthie inspected the trout on her hook. It had taken her fifteen minutes just to reel it in. The battle between her and the giant fish had been one of epic proportions. The kind of battle that sportsmen tell around campfires. Like her dad's favorite story, *The Old Man and the Sea,* or David fighting Goliath.

Using the space between her forefinger's first and second knuckle as a measuring stick, Ruthie measured the fish from head to tail. *Eleven inches!* she noted. *Grandpa Charles would be proud.*

She tossed the pole over her shoulder and began the long walk to her cabin. The smelly fish hung behind her, still on the line, dangling just inches above her feet.

A few minutes later, Ruthie passed a sign pointing the way to her cabin. She felt her excitement rise. She was free of her family for the first time in her life!

Suddenly, she hopped for no reason at

all. Then the hopping turned into skipping.

"Skipper," she said aloud. "That's the name of my fish. Skipper!"

Ruthie spotted a big log lying crosswise on the trail. It was the perfect opportunity to jump. To jump as high and as far as she could.

Ruthie held tight to her fishing pole, then bent down like she was preparing for a long-jump contest. *One, two . . .* , she counted. *Three!*

Ruthie ran, leaped, and cleared the log by over a foot. She turned around to make sure the fish was still there. It was. Skipper had jumped with her.

The trail began to wind, and Ruthie now imagined herself behind the wheel of a race car. She zoomed along the winding trail, her feet running as fast as Fred Flintstone's, until she arrived at a long, skinny cabin.

A wisp of smoke was coming from the chimney, as though a fire had just been started.

Ruthie opened the heavy wooden door and looked inside. A dozen girls, already unpacked and situated, were chattering away on their bunk beds. As soon as they saw Ruthie's fish, they squealed like frightened piglets.

Ruthie laughed. She liked it when girls acted silly. It made her appreciate how cool she was. She liked being different. It was way more fun than being normal.

A short, punchy girl jumped down off her bunk bed and marched up to Ruthie. She wasn't afraid of the fish. "Did you catch that yourself?" she demanded.

Ruthie liked her straightforward attitude. "Yep."

The girl, whose name was Bailey, held out a flat open palm. Ruthie slapped it as hard as she could. Bailey nodded, impressed. Then she pointed to an empty bunk bed, right under her own.

"Make yourself comfy."

A perky redheaded girl yelped, "Don't come in with that thing!"

Ruthie shrugged. "What should I do with it?"

Bailey's eyes lit up, and she grabbed Ruthie's hand. "Let's cook it! There's a barbecue grill right outside!"

A freckle-faced girl put her hands on her hips and quipped, "Not without our counselor's permission."

"Yeah," a skinny one chirped. "And she's in the bathroom."

Bailey rolled her eyes at Ruthie.

"Permission-smishen!" she declared, tossing the girls' concerns aside with a sweep of her hand. "I've got matches in my bag."

FIVE

Downstairs at the Camdens', everybody was talking about Simon. Matt sat across the table from his father. Slurping his cereal, he began complaining, ticking off his list of grievances like a lawyer pleading to a jury.

"I took a week off from my summer studies to spend time with the family," he said, holding up his forefinger.

"I moved back into the house while the girls are gone," he explained, adding his second finger to the count.

"I've planned a whole week of activities." Up went the third finger.

"And Simon doesn't have a moment to spend with his big brother?" Matt's mouth was wide open, unable to believe that "little" Simon was now big enough to have his own life.

Reverend Camden smiled. "I'm proud of him."

Matt leaned back in his chair, annoyed that his father was taking Simon's side.

The reverend continued, clearly excited by Simon's new project. He began reciting his own list.

"He's turned an unknown after-school club into a success." The first finger popped up.

"He's mentoring younger students." The second finger rose.

"He's won the respect of his teacher." Reverend Camden smiled as he held the three fingers up in front of Matt.

But the proud father wasn't finished. A fourth finger went up and he waved all four at Matt like a victory flag. "And *four*— this could be the beginning of a lifelong career for Simon. I think you need to support him, even if it's ruined your plans."

Across the room, Mrs. Camden, who'd been doing some thinking of her own, nodded as she opened the refrigerator. "I think we should let Simon invest a small portion of our family savings."

Her husband's four fingers fell to the table. He turned around in his chair and looked at his wife in shock.

"Invest *our* savings?" he asked, just to make sure he had heard her correctly.

"A small portion. Absolutely." Mrs. Camden's voice was certain as she pulled out a carton of milk.

But Reverend Camden's smile had frozen—supporting their son's hobby was one thing, but letting him take the family's financial future into his own hands was quite another.

"If somebody's going to invest our money, I think it should be one of us," he told his wife firmly.

Mrs. Camden poured herself a glass of milk, but didn't say anything.

The reverend looked at her, hoping she would nod in agreement. She didn't.

Then he looked at Matt. But Matt wasn't getting involved. After all, his dad hadn't taken his side earlier.

Now Reverend Camden felt defensive. "Just because I'm a minister doesn't mean I'm a financial idiot!" he exclaimed.

Mrs. Camden took a drink of her milk,

trying to hide her smile. "Is that why we have a smaller savings account than your little sister?" she asked.

Offended, the reverend retorted, "Julie doesn't have seven kids."

Mrs. Camden nodded. "I'm not saying that you've mismanaged our money. I'm just saying that we should give Simon a shot."

Matt quietly stood up from his chair and tiptoed out of the kitchen.

The next morning, Lucy and Sabrina dressed for the day in silence. That is, until Sabrina's cell phone rang again. Just as she had done the afternoon before, Sabrina walked as far away from Lucy as possible to talk.

Curious, Lucy struggled to hear what Sabrina was saying, but couldn't. *It's probably her boyfriend, or a big modeling agent.*

Frustrated by Sabrina's cool attitude, Lucy made a promise to herself as she slipped on her sport shorts. She was going to get Sabrina to talk by the end of the day—even if it was about something stupid, like clothes.

Twenty minutes later, the two girls

walked down the trail toward the quad. The Welcoming Games were beginning in half an hour. Lucy considered asking Sabrina about her modeling, but it felt too awkward. She was sure that everybody asked Sabrina what it was like to be on the page of a magazine. She probably hated talking about it.

As they walked, Lucy noticed that dozens of guys were flocking around them. Their behavior was always the same: they would hurry to catch up with the two girls, then slow down just in front of Sabrina. Then they'd shove each other around, glance back toward her, and grin.

Lucy knew they were showing off for Sabrina, who rarely looked their way. Then something occurred to Lucy. Something that was so obvious, and yet so easy to miss. *Nobody treats Sabrina like a normal person.*

The thought was enough to help Lucy break through Sabrina's ice. The perfect place to start was with the cell phone.

"So who's the mysterious caller?" she asked, and was happily surprised at how casual she sounded. *Like the old Lucy. Like the confident Lucy.*

Sabrina's voice was soft when she spoke. "A doctor."

Lucy looked at Sabrina, who was looking at the ground as she walked. *Maybe she'd prefer not to discuss this,* Lucy thought. But then a braver idea occurred to her.

Maybe she *wanted* to talk to somebody, but didn't know how. Suddenly, Lucy realized that her roommate might actually need her friendship.

"Is everything okay?" Lucy asked.

Sabrina shook her head. "It's my little sister. She's very sick."

Just then, a group of girl counselors walked up behind them. They were clustered together like a gaggle of geese.

Lucy turned around to greet them— but before she could say hello, they rolled their eyes at Sabrina, then pushed their noses up with their forefingers and walked right by. Tara was right in the middle of the group. Practically leading them.

As soon as they passed Lucy and Sabrina, the girls burst out laughing and ran down toward the grassy quad.

Sabrina turned to Lucy. Her soft demeanor suddenly hardened. "I know that people talk about me, Lucy. But they don't know me."

Lucy nodded and said gently, "That's *why* they talk. Because they *don't* know you. And because you don't go out of your way to let them."

Sabrina looked down at the gang of girls. "At least I'm not mean."

Lucy smiled. "You're right. You're not mean at all. You convinced Mrs. Stout to give me my stereo back—and I really appreciate it. But when I tried to thank you . . ."

Lucy looked at Sabrina, uncertain if she should finish her thought. After all, she barely knew the girl. But Sabrina's face was open and earnest, as though she wanted to hear Lucy's criticism.

"You were cold and distant," Lucy finished.

Sabrina sighed. "I know, I know. But I was nervous."

Lucy laughed. "Nervous? About meeting *me*?"

Lucy was shocked when Sabrina nodded.

"I was terrified. I saw you on the bus with Tara, and then I saw her point to me and whisper. She hates me. Everybody hates me."

"That's not true."

"It is true."

Lucy realized she couldn't argue with Sabrina. When it came to the girls at camp, she was probably right. They did hate her. *Maybe I can talk to Tara and convince her that Sabrina's not so bad.*

"I wanted this year to be different," Sabrina explained. "Before I walked into the cabin yesterday, I stood outside and thought about what I'd tell you. How I'm not this awful person. And when I finally got the courage to walk in and introduce myself . . ."

Sabrina threw up her hands in exasperation as she completed the thought. "There was *Dirk*!"

The name caught Lucy off guard. "Wait a minute. Are you telling me that you like *Dirk Porter*?"

Sabrina clapped her hand over Lucy's mouth, grinning. "Shhh!"

Lucy hid her disappointment with a smile.

There go my chances, Lucy thought.

She put her arm around Sabrina, realizing that even if she'd lost her go at a great guy, she'd definitely gained a new friend. Looking at Sabrina with an air of mischief, Lucy asked: "Want me to find out if he likes you?"

Five minutes later, Lucy was in a crowd of campers on the quad. Dirk and his roommate, Robin—a tall blond with broad shoulders—stood in the center of the group, addressing them. They explained the rules for the first Welcoming Game, which was called Capture the Flag.

"There will be two teams," Dirk announced into a large orange megaphone. "My team and Robin's team."

Dirk looked at his own team, who were already picked and standing before him. They all wore green hats. Then he pointed to the woods in front of them. "Our flag is hidden in that forest. It's our job to protect it from the evil enemy, the Orange Ogres."

A hiss from his team went up as he handed the megaphone to Robin. Robin looked at his team, who were wearing orange hats. His brown eyes narrowed in mock seriousness as he pointed to the woods behind them. "Our flag is hidden in this forest. We must never surrender it to the Green Goblins."

His team hissed at Dirk's team as a hand shot up in the crowd. Robin nodded for the boy to speak.

"But how do we get their flag if we're guarding ours?"

Robin smiled at his curiosity. "Good question. Each team will be split into two groups," he explained. "One group will guard their flag, and the other group will go in search of the enemy's. Does that make sense?"

All the campers nodded. Except for one. The same boy. "But how do you win?" he asked.

Robin handed the megaphone to Dirk, who pointed to a large circle drawn in the middle of the quad. "This is home base. If you can get the opposing team's flag back here without getting tagged by them, then you win."

"But what happens if you get tagged?" the boy pressed.

Dirk grinned. "Then you get sent to home base, where you have to sit out the rest of the game."

A loud cry of "Boo!" went up. Clearly,

nobody wanted to get stuck at home base.

Dirk held the megaphone back up. "I'll monitor my enemy's team to make sure no one cheats." Then he narrowed his eyes at Robin and playfully raised a fist at him. "If I bust any Orange Ogres, back to base they go."

A low murmur of "Ooh!" came from Dirk's team members, who were excited to compete against Robin's team.

Robin took the megaphone, turned to his team, and motioned toward Dirk. He puffed up his chest like an overgrown muscle man strutting in front of an audience. His team started laughing. Everybody was enjoying the competitive banter between the two game leaders.

Then Robin looked out at the group of teachers and counselors. "Does anybody want to tag up with us as monitors?"

Several hands—all female—went up. Lucy's hand was among them. She was hoping that Dirk would pick her so she could find out if he liked Sabrina. But before Dirk had a chance, Robin pointed right at Lucy and smiled.

A few minutes later, Lucy and Robin were

walking through the woods, waiting for the whistle to blow and the game to begin.

Up close, Lucy realized that Robin was quite attractive. He wasn't as charming or boisterous as Dirk, but he had other great qualities. Besides his obvious good looks, he was intelligent, expressive, and a good listener.

Lucy decided to ask him about Sabrina. "Do you know if Dirk likes my roommate?" she asked.

Robin quickly retorted, "Why? Do you like Dirk?"

Uh-oh, Lucy thought, sensing a change in Robin's energy. There was tension in the air, but she wasn't sure why. Then it hit her. *Robin likes me.*

He put his hands in his pockets, and looked straight at Lucy, unafraid.

"Well, do you?"

Lucy shook her head and lied. "No, why?"

Robin smiled and raised a playful eyebrow. "Are you sure?"

Lucy laughed. "Of course I'm sure."

"And why not?" Robin pressed. He was definitely flirting with her. Maybe he even wanted her to say, *Because I like you, Robin.*

But before she could decide whether or not to take the bait, the whistle sounded, cutting the conversation short. The games were on—and Lucy didn't know if she was disappointed or relieved.

SIX

Luckily for Ruthie, Bailey had been unable to find her matches and the fish was still not fried. Now the two girls were sneaking through the woods, trying to find their enemy's flag.

"You know what's really cool?" Ruthie whispered to Bailey as they slunk behind a tree.

"Me," Bailey said.

Ruthie laughed. "Besides us."

Bailey shrugged. "What?"

Ruthie pointed to the hat on her head. "We got on the team with green hats. We're camouflaged."

Bailey's eyes lit up, and she pulled her

cap down as low as it would go. "Yeah. No one can see us!"

Ruthie got down on her knees and Bailey followed her lead. They crawled to the next tree and then stood up behind it. They peeked out around the tree, scanning for any sign of an orange flag or enemy scouts. They saw neither.

"Imagine if you had to wear an orange hat like those losers on the other team," Ruthie snickered. "That's like wearing a big neon sign that says, *I'm right here!*"

Bailey snorted in agreement. In a flash, a boy in an orange hat jumped out from behind a tree. "You didn't see me!" he growled, about to tag them.

Before they could get a good look at him, the two girls were off and running.

Ruthie's legs flew so fast she felt like an Olympic sprinter. She leaped over a log, dashed behind a tree, ducked beneath a bush, and rolled out the other side. Then she realized Bailey was not behind her.

Suddenly, there was a rustle in the bush. The boy wasn't chasing after Bailey. He was coming after Ruthie!

That's when she got a brilliant idea.

She grabbed a few rocks. Up ahead was the trail to her cabin, and just beyond it was a slight drop-off. . . .

She took off running again, but this time in the boy's plain sight. She heard his footsteps rush in behind her, and grinned.

She ran straight across the trail, around a curve, and for the drop-off, seeing it was shallow enough for her to jump into without getting hurt. On the other side of the drop, she could see that the forest was dense and easy to hide in.

She leaped off the drop and tumbled into a bed of leaves below. She did a back roll into the belly of an overhanging rock formation. Then she crouched there, hidden from above by the overhang.

She heard footsteps running overhead. Then the boy leaped off the drop, tumbling headlong into the leaves. That's when she threw the rocks into the dark forest before her. She threw them as far as she could.

When the boy pulled himself up, his ears were drawn to the sound of the rustling branches. Certain the noise was caused by Ruthie's feet, he chased after the sound as his orange hat fell behind him.

Ruthie had to cover her mouth to keep from laughing. But then she stopped when she recognized his blond hair. She had seen the boy before. He was the cute kid from the bus, the one who had pulled her curls.

She picked up his hat. At first she considered going after him. The hat would be a good excuse to talk to him—and to see if he was as cute up close as he was from a bouncing bus seat.

But then she thought better of it. She could *wear* the orange hat and the enemy would think she was on their team. They would tell her exactly where the flag was hidden. She could use the hat to win the game!

And win it, she did.

After the Welcoming Games were over, Lucy realized that she still hadn't found out if Dirk liked Sabrina. All she had learned was that Robin liked her.

Moments later, Dirk asked Lucy to walk back to camp with him. She was sure she knew why—he wanted her to play matchmaker for him and Sabrina. Little did he know, she was already formulating a plan of action for *everybody*. The last thing she wanted was to be a third wheel.

"I had a great time with Robin," she said, glancing casually at Dirk. "He's a great guy. In fact, I was thinking, if everybody's game, that maybe you and he might want to double-date with Sabrina and me."

Dirk looked at her and smiled. He was definitely hip to that plan.

"That'd be cool," he said.

Lucy felt like patting herself on the back. She had handled it all very smoothly, and had gotten a clear answer for Sabrina without any confusing complications.

"Great!" Lucy exclaimed. "How about tomorrow night at the Campfire Gathering?"

Dirk reached up and touched Lucy's face. "How about right now?"

Before Lucy could react, he kissed her.

Lucy pulled away, her heart suddenly pounding. She struggled to get the right words out. "I meant that you should date Sabrina," she said, breathless.

Dirk's confident smile faded. He was confused. "Why? Do you like Robin?"

Lucy shook her head. "No. But Sabrina likes you."

Dirk started laughing, and Lucy remembered what it was about him that she had found so attractive yesterday in the cabin.

It was his laugh, his sense of humor. It welled up and then exploded, as though it were coming from a place deep inside. Sure, he was gorgeous—but what set him apart from all the other good-looking guys Lucy had known was this one simple thing. His laugh.

"That's really funny," he said. "Because Robin likes Sabrina."

Lucy's jaw dropped. "Sabrina?"

Dirk nodded. Now it was her turn to laugh. She had completely misread Robin's interest in her. The only reason he had wanted to know if she liked Dirk was because *Dirk* liked Lucy all along!

"So let me get this straight," she said, taking a step back. "Robin likes Sabrina, Sabrina likes you, and you like *me*?"

Dirk noticed the emphasis Lucy placed on the word *me* and nodded. He cut straight to the chase. "Sabrina's a very pretty girl, Lucy. But I want more than just looks. I want a girl who knows who she is, and who knows what she wants. I knew the first second I met you that you were that girl."

Lucy shook her head, confused by her memories of their first meeting. "But you were so nervous when Sabrina walked into the cabin yesterday."

"I was nervous because of *you*. And because I had a feeling that Sabrina liked me . . . and I didn't want you to get the wrong idea. I just wanted to get out of there—and wait until I could see you again, alone, and tell you how I felt."

Lucy couldn't believe it. It was all too good to be true. "Well, w-what about . . . ," she stammered, looking into his eyes. *They're so gorgeous. So green. I could get way too lost in those eyes.*

"What about what?" he asked.

"Sabrina?" she finally finished.

Dirk shrugged. "We'll set her up with Robin."

Lucy shook her head. "She'd never go for it. She likes you."

Dirk grinned suddenly, his bright eyes bubbling with mischief. "Then we'll have to make her like him."

Lucy's brow furrowed in confusion. "Make her like him?"

Dirk nodded. "Tomorrow night, Sabrina and I are the only teachers who aren't on campfire duty. If you can convince her to come by and visit me during my off-duty hours, then I can switch duties with Robin."

Lucy reasoned his thoughts out loud. "You mean she'll think she's going to visit you, but then Robin will answer the door— and you won't be there?"

Dirk nodded. "Then they'll realize they're the only two teachers not on duty. And if Robin's smooth enough, he'll convince her to hang out."

Lucy grinned in spite of herself. She liked where the idea was headed. She liked it a lot. She was going to play matchmaker after all!

Back at the Camdens', Simon was getting more business than he'd anticipated.

Mrs. Camden walked into his new office and pulled up a chair. She looked at him as he typed away on his borrowed computer. She was certain she was making the right decision.

"I want to cut a deal with you," she said in almost a whisper.

Simon perked up. "A deal?" *Deal* was his favorite word in the English language.

Mrs. Camden nodded. "Your father and I have been talking about letting you invest a *tiny* percentage of our family savings."

Simon's eyes widened. "Seriously? You *and* Dad want me to invest the family savings?"

"*I* want you to. Your dad doesn't. He thinks you're too green to handle our money. And he may be right."

Simon was practically jumping out of his seat. "I'm absolutely ready to do this! I'm begging you to let me do this!"

Mrs. Camden held up her hand, directing him to calm down. "I've decided to take out three hundred dollars from my own personal savings account, rather than from the family account."

Simon clapped, "That's perfect! Three hundred dollars can definitely get us started—"

His mother cut him off. "First explain to me how it works. Do you have a plan already?"

Simon nodded eagerly. "Here's what I'll do: I'll divide the money into three equal portions, then invest it in three separate hot stocks."

"Hot stocks?"

Simon nodded. "Stocks that analysts predict will have an immediate spike."

"Spike?" Mrs. Camden asked.

"A rise. For example, if we buy a stock for thirty dollars, and it spikes the next day, then the stock could be worth, say, forty dollars."

Mrs. Camden nodded. It all made sense so far. "And then what happens?"

Simon continued. "If all three stocks spike the day after we invest, then we pull the money out and *bingo!* Profit!"

Mrs. Camden was energized by her son's zeal. But she was also cautious. "And what if they don't spike?"

"That's why we split the money between stocks," Simon explained. "It lowers your risk by upping your odds. So if I invest in three hot stocks, but one doesn't rise in value, you're covered—because the odds are that the other two will rise. You'll still make a profit."

"And you know which stocks will rise?" Mrs. Camden questioned, excited to learn from her son.

"The analysts make suggestions based on research about various companies. And I do my own research to be sure," said Simon with confidence. "It's like anything in life. Nothing guarantees you'll win, but if you educate yourself, you shift the odds in your favor."

Mrs. Camden considered his logic. It sounded solid. And something inside her was certain that she could trust Simon. "How much do you think we can make?" she asked.

"Maybe sixty bucks."

Mrs. Camden calculated in her head. "That's twenty percent of the initial investment. That's good."

Simon clearly agreed. "My advice to you is to let me invest the three hundred dollars as I see fit, and then when you make the sixty dollars, pull the three hundred out—and put it back in the bank, where it's safe. Then let me reinvest the sixty."

Mrs. Camden smiled, understanding her son's logic. "That way if we ever lose the sixty, we really haven't lost anything. The three hundred is still safe in the bank. That's very smart, Simon."

Simon leaned toward his mother. "Have you told Dad you've decided to do this?"

Mrs. Camden shook her head. "No. But it's my own money. It's not like I'm risking his savings."

Simon grinned. He liked that his mother was being a little sneaky. The older he got, the more he recognized this quality in both of his parents. It was funny.

Mrs. Camden noticed the mischievous look in her son's eye. She shook her head. "For the record, I'm not doing this to be devious. I've decided to put any profit that I make into the family account. I'm doing it to help you kids, and to help Dad—who has a bad time handling money."

Simon grinned and stuck out his hand to shake. "I won't tell him."

Mrs. Camden laughed as she shook his hand. "It's not a secret, Simon!"

But Simon noted that she whispered the word *secret*. This was definitely confidential information.

Little did they know, Reverend Camden stood in the hallway, his back plastered against the wall, eavesdropping on the conversation. Then he sneaked away quietly, tiptoeing down the stairs—and chuckling softly to himself.

SEVEN

The next morning, Lucy was cutting her own kind of deal. She and Sabrina were both sitting up in bed, discussing the previous night's events. Lucy chose her words very carefully.

"Before I could ask Dirk if he liked you, he told me that he liked another girl."

Sabrina slumped in her bed. She sighed and pulled the covers up under her chin.

Lucy held up her hand. "Don't get bummed yet. Keep listening." Sabrina nodded, a slight flicker of hope in her eyes.

Lucy continued. "So instead of asking him about you, when I knew his mind was on this other person, I came up with a plan."

Sabrina's eyes narrowed. "A plan?"

Lucy nodded, enthusiastic about the strategy she and Dirk had worked out. "You have to hear me out."

Sabrina couldn't help but laugh at Lucy's eagerness. It was contagious. "Okay, I'll listen."

Lucy rubbed her hands together, took a breath, and began. "Tonight is the Campfire Gathering. And if you'll take a look at your duty roster, you'll notice that—"

Sabrina cut her off. "I'm not on duty, and neither is Dirk."

"Exactly!" Lucy said

Sabrina rolled her eyes. "Which means I won't be able to see him at all."

Lucy jumped out of her bed and dived across the room into Sabrina's. "Wrongo, Sabrina! Put on your thinking cap! It means you'll get to see him while he's *alone!*"

Sabrina looked sideways at Lucy. How could she see Dirk if his cabin was on the other side of the woods?

"Dirk told me he's staying in his cabin tonight, all by himself!"

"And . . . ?" Sabrina asked cautiously.

"He's going to be bored out of his mind!"

Sabrina shrugged. She wasn't nearly as pumped about Lucy's plan as Lucy was. In fact, she didn't fully understand it. "Are you saying I should ask him out? Because there's no way I'm going to do that!"

"I'm saying you should go visit him, right after Robin has left."

"No way!"

"Yes way!"

Sabrina stared at Lucy. She really was crazy. "What do I say? 'Would you like to buy some Girl Scout cookies?'"

Lucy crossed her arms. "You haven't heard me out. I have a plan for everything."

Sabrina crossed her arms and leaned back in her bed, skeptical. "So start talking."

Lucy grinned. "I don't know if you've noticed Dirk's roommate or not, but he's off-the-Richter-scale *hot*."

Sabrina jumped in. "You have a crush!"

"No!" Lucy protested.

"Yes, you do!"

Lucy shrugged, refusing to divulge.

"The point is, I'm stopping by their cabin at eight to pick him up for the Campfire Gathering."

"I bet you are!" Sabrina teased.

Lucy sighed like a mother annoyed with a child. She looked down her nose at Sabrina to make sure she was paying attention. She was. "At eight-fifteen, *you* are going to stop by looking for *me*."

Sabrina's gleaming eyes turned somber. "Why?"

Lucy rolled her eyes. Didn't this girl have any imagination? "Because my mother just called and needs to talk to me, because I have your cell phone in my pocket, because you just found the jacket I was looking for . . . who cares? Just make up an excuse!"

The wheels in Sabrina's head started turning. Now she was getting into it. "I like the cell phone excuse!"

Lucy smiled. "It's all yours."

Sabrina started to rock on her bed, having caught Lucy's energy bug. "And then what?"

"Robin and I will be long gone, of course. And you'll be standing face to face with Dirk."

Finally, Sabrina grinned. "And that's when I make my move!"

Sabrina's face lit up in a way Lucy wouldn't have imagined possible just a day ago. The cold, sophisticated mask she wore for the world had vanished.

Lucy bit her lip. Beneath all her excitement and anticipation was an emotion she had tried all night to ignore: guilt. She prayed that the plan wouldn't backfire.

On the other side of camp, Dirk was having an easier time convincing Robin to join in their matchmaking plan.

The two guys sat across from one another at the table, munching on cereal. Dirk was coaching Robin in the game of love.

"You, my friend, have to woo this girl like you've never wooed a girl before."

Robin shrugged. "I'm not really the wooing type," he began. "I think people should just be direct."

Dirk laughed. "Yeah, you've been so direct you've never said a single word to her."

Robin shrugged again. "She makes me nervous."

Dirk shook his head. "You've gotta make things happen."

Robin held up his hands in defense. "I've got my own brand of charm—it's natural. Not manufactured. And that takes time."

Dirk sat back in his chair, amused. "Really."

Robin nodded. "Listen, Don Juan. I'm a true-blue Romeo."

Dirk laughed. "Good. You need to be. Sabrina's had a wicked crush on me for *years*."

Robin shrugged off Dirk's playful taunting. "So what's the plan?"

Dirk proceeded. "She thinks she's coming by to see *me*, so you have to intercept her and convince her that you're the guy she really wants to hang with."

Robin reached across the table and shoved Dirk's rumpled bedhead. "That shouldn't be a problem. I mean, look at you. . . ."

Dirk grabbed the round plastic lid of the milk jug. This was war. He set the lid down on the table, then motioned for Robin to compete in his game of table soccer. "You think this is gonna be a real piece of cake, don't you?"

Robin took the bait and stationed his hands, palms out, against his edge of the table. He grinned. "I know you're the 'King of Camp,' but I just might have to overthrow you."

Dirk narrowed his eyes, pulled in his middle finger, aimed at the plastic milk lid, and flicked it as hard as he could toward the outer edge of the table.

Robin's hands darted down the table, deflecting the lid, which ricocheted off his palms and landed in Dirk's cereal bowl.

Dirk fetched the lid out, wiped it on his pants, and set it back on the table.

Robin pointed at his pants. "Case in point. You're dirty. You just wiped milk on your pants."

Dirk laughed. "All right, all right. I'm a little messy, and you're good at defense. I'll give you that." He slid the lid over to Robin's side. "But the game of love, my friend, isn't a defensive game. It's about offense. You've gotta have a plan or the girl will get away."

Robin nodded, then positioned the lid

as Dirk's hand guards went up across the table. Robin pretended to aim toward the outer right edge, just as Dirk had done. He waited until Dirk's hands crept in that direction, then flicked right toward the center of the table.

But Dirk's hands were too fast. The lid deflected off his palms, and Robin slumped momentarily. Dirk noted his roommate's creeping doubt. He took the lid and put it back on the plastic milk jug. Then he leaned across the table to give his friend some advice.

"Here's what I know about Sabrina: she's shy."

Robin cocked his head. "Shy? Sabrina Van Raming is *shy*?"

Dirk nodded. "It comes off as confidence, but it's really just her way of protecting herself from people she's afraid to talk to."

Robin looked at his roommate with a new sense of respect. Underneath all that jockish bravado was an insightful guy. Maybe he was right about Sabrina— maybe she was shy.

"So what do I do?" Robin asked.

Dirk shrugged. "The best thing a guy

can do for a girl is listen to her."

Robin looked more confused than ever. "But if she's too shy to talk, then what am I going to listen to?"

Dirk shook his head. This guy didn't have a clue. "You have to ask her questions. What's her family like, what music does she dig, that sort of stuff."

Robin nodded. "I can do that," he said. "I've wondered all of those things about Sabrina anyway." Suddenly, a thought occurred to him. "What do I say when she asks where you are?"

Dirk smiled as he leaned back in his seat. He and Lucy had already thought of everything. "You tell her that you just found out your brother broke his leg—"

Robin shook his head, interrupting Dirk. "I don't have a brother."

"Then your sister—"

Robin interrupted again. "I don't have a—"

Exasperated, Dirk cut him off. "The point is to gain her sympathy so she'll hang out with you. Tell her somebody in your family broke a leg, and you were too worried to go out—so I took your campfire duty. Now you're waiting in your cabin so they'll know where to find you in case a phone call comes. And you'd love her to come in and sit with you."

Robin nodded. He wasn't crazy about lying to the girl he adored, but he couldn't deny that the plan was solid. How could he fail?

Meanwhile, at the Camdens', Mrs. Camden was standing outside a closed door, enjoying the drama that was unfolding in Simon's office.

Inside, her husband was privately cutting his own deal with Simon. He held out three hundred dollars, motioning for his son to take it.

"I want you to invest this in a little company called TimeStar," he said.

Simon guffawed. "TimeStar?! You want to invest in a company that hasn't turned a profit in three years? They're so in the red they can't *pay* people to take their stock!"

Reverend Camden sat down on the desk. "Well, I happen to know their vice president, and he is a very smart man. He's certain that things are about to change. He told me himself."

Simon stared at his father in disbelief. "It's in his own *self-interest* to convince you to buy his company's stock. That's where they get their operating money. Without suckers like you, the company would fold."

The reverend stood up and wobbled his head back and forth like a turkey. "Well, well. I guess you think, like your mom does, that I don't know anything about investing. But I know a lot more than you two think I do, Mr. Smarty-Pants. And I want you to invest in TimeStar."

Simon sighed. "Why don't you just invest yourself then? I don't want to be responsible for your loss."

Reverend Camden shrugged nonchalantly. "Because I don't want to deal with an agent."

Simon cracked a smile. "You mean a broker?"

The reverend nodded. "That's what I said. A broker."

Simon stood up and put his arm around his dad. He leaned in and whispered, "I know that all this new technology, the gizmos, the lingo, is a bit unsettling for your generation. But you need to trust me on this. I know what I'm doing. Don't invest in TimeStar."

Reverend Camden narrowed his eyes at his uppity son. "*My generation*, huh? Let me tell you something: *my generation* bore and raised your generation. Without us, you kids wouldn't have had the resources with which to create this marvelous, cold, alienating cyberworld of yours. Now invest my money in TimeStar, and invest it all."

Simon raised his hands, giving in to his father's wishes. "Fine. But I have to demand a brokerage fee of fifteen dollars. Seven for the cost of the trade, and eight as my fee."

Reverend Camden protested. "You didn't charge your mom a fee!"

Simon grinned. "How do you know? Were you listening at the door?"

The reverend's fatherly expression melted into a guarded smile. He was busted and he knew it. "I happened to pass by, yes. And you didn't charge her a fee."

Simon nodded. "Because she let *me* invest her money as *I* saw fit—she believes in *my* abilities. *You're* doing this to get back at her for going behind your back!"

Reverend Camden began to protest, then realized that Simon was right again. He reluctantly pulled out his wallet and retrieved fifteen dollars. "So I'm competing with your mother. But it's all in good fun, and I know she'd say the same thing." Then he smiled. "And I'm going to win!"

EIGHT

Down at the quad, a ten-foot bonfire was burning. Kids milled about. The night was warm enough for shorts and T-shirts. Around the campfire stood counselors and teachers, some playing acoustic guitars, others leading the campers in a round of singing.

Lucy glanced at her watch. It was almost eight-thirty. If Sabrina and Robin had hit it off, it would have happened by now.

She glanced at Dirk, who stood beside her. She motioned with her eyes toward an opening in the crowd. If they sneaked away now, they could peek in on Robin's cabin—and see if Sabrina had stayed or gone.

Dirk nodded; then Lucy leaned over and whispered, "Tara said she'll cover for me."

Dirk took her hand. "Perfect. Mike's got my back, so we should be fine."

Lucy agreed, and the two started to slip out toward the woods. That is, until a little voice squawked behind them.

"Sneaking away, huh?"

Lucy turned to discover Ruthie, with her arms crossed and her eyebrows raised, gloating behind her. "Look who's not behaving," the delighted girl crooned.

Lucy smiled and pinched her little sister's nose. "The counselors and teachers have permission to leave in rotating fifteen-minute shifts, so long as someone is covering for us. It's our turn."

Ruthie's glee dissipated. "Oh." But then her eyes fell to Lucy's hand, which was entwined with Dirk's. The glee reappeared. "And who's this?"

Lucy put her arm around Dirk. "This is Dirk. Dirk, this is my little sister, Ruthie."

Dirk extended his hand to shake, but

instead of shaking back, Ruthie slid her hand quickly along his in a hip exchange of skin. Then she looked him up and down, from his soccer sneakers to his shiny black hair.

"Are you her new boyfriend?" she demanded.

Lucy's hand shot straight up to Dirk's mouth, covering it quickly. "You don't have to answer that," she said.

Just then, Ruthie felt a tug on one of her curls. She whipped around as a blond streak ran by, disappearing in the crowd.

Lucy smiled down at her, enjoying her turn at gloating. "Is that *your* new boyfriend?"

Moments later, Lucy and Dirk sneaked up to a large cabin window and peered in. With a quiet high five, they noted that Sabrina was inside the room! She was sitting at the table, across from Robin, who appeared to be doing all the talking.

Lucy strained to hear, but the window was closed. She looked at Dirk, who motioned toward an open window on the other side of the cabin.

Lucy looked skeptical. "It's right under

the outside light," she whispered. "They'll see us."

Dirk shook his head, took Lucy's hand, and dropped to his hands and knees. Lucy followed his lead, and the two began crawling around the base of the cabin.

But just before they reached the window, they saw an obstacle in front of them. A bed of jade bushes, too thick to crawl through, grew like a fence outside the window. They would have to sneak over the bushes and risk being seen in the light.

Dirk stood up and hopped over them as silently and quickly as a cat. He dropped back to his knees, then waved at Lucy to do the same.

Unfortunately, Lucy's legs were shorter than Dirk's. She would have to jump higher to clear the bushes. She positioned herself on her haunches, then sprang up over the greenery.

Her head cracked loudly against an overhanging pine branch. She dropped to her knees as Sabrina's and Robin's eyes darted toward the window.

Trying not to laugh while simultaneously trying not to cry, Lucy held her hand over her mouth. Dirk mouthed, "You okay?" Lucy nodded, and Dirk leaned over and kissed the top of her head.

The two crouched in silence, wondering if Robin and Sabrina had seen or heard them. If they had, Lucy noted, they weren't discussing it. In fact, it didn't sound like they were discussing anything. Lucy nervously looked at Dirk, who whispered, "Maybe they're kissing?"

Lucy shook her head, certain that things hadn't changed so abruptly in a few seconds. She bit her lip, worried that things weren't going well.

Finally, they heard Robin's voice.

"My little sister didn't really break her leg," he said. There was another long silence.

Lucy cringed and Dirk hit his forehead in a gesture of stupidity. It didn't sound like Robin was getting very far.

"I lied to gain your sympathy," Robin finally added.

Dirk hit his forehead harder, and Lucy shook her head, certain that the affair was doomed.

There was another long silence, this one more interminable than the last.

Finally, Robin spoke again. "I hope

you don't hate me," he offered.

Lucy rolled her eyes and leaned in to Dirk. "Is this how you coached him to woo a girl?" she whispered.

Dirk shook his head and held up his palm as though swearing to the truth. "I told him to lie!" he whispered back.

Lucy laughed, suddenly hearing the scolding voice of her mother. *"I guess that's what you get then, isn't it?"*

Dirk held his hand up quickly to quiet her, then motioned toward the window. Robin was saying something else.

"I didn't know how else to convince you to hang out with me tonight. I . . . I really like you, Sabrina."

The two Peeping Toms held their breath, praying for a positive reaction. When Sabrina finally spoke, her voice was soft and confused. *"You* like me?"

Lucy and Dirk crept slowly upward toward the window and peered inside. Robin was nodding his head.

"I've always liked you, since the first year you came to camp. But I never knew how to ask you out—I didn't think you'd ever go out with me."

There was another long silence.

Sabrina put her head in her hands as though uncertain of how to react, uncertain of how to feel. Robin waited, nervous.

Sabrina finally looked up. To his surprise, she smiled. But her eyes, which had been focused on him until just moments ago, were now detached and cool. "You didn't switch duties with Dirk by accident, did you?"

Robin's eyes fell to the table, his hopeful expression fading. He bit his lip, knowing he should be honest—but also knowing that admitting the truth was the same as digging his own grave. "No, I didn't. . . ."

Sabrina's voice hardened. "Which means he and Lucy are in on this."

Robin nodded—even though she hadn't asked him a question. She had stated a fact.

"And that other girl that Dirk likes . . . ," Sabrina began. "What's her name?"

Robin leaned forward in his seat. "I know it sounds bad—"

"It's Lucy, isn't it?"

Robin looked down at the table again. It was all the answer that Sabrina needed.

Outside the window, Lucy sank down

onto the ground. She felt sick to her stomach. She should have known this would happen. She should have just been honest from the beginning.

Inside, Robin confessed everything. "Don't be mad at them. Be mad at me for going along with a plan that they made up *for me*. They did it because they care about me, and they care about you. They wanted us to get together. . . ."

Sabrina crossed her arms. "No. They did it for *them*. They wanted to get together without feeling guilty about hurting me. They used *both* of us to make them feel better about their choices and about their deception. I think that's pretty clear."

Robin was shocked at Sabrina's words, perhaps because he knew they were true. Or maybe because she was a lot smarter than he'd ever imagined.

Sabrina crossed her arms and looked down at the floor. She was mad. She felt used and manipulated by the two people she liked the most at camp. The *only* people she liked at camp.

Robin reached out and took her hand. "Can I hold your hand?"

Sabrina snorted and pulled her hand

away. "Hold my hand? After you've plotted with your friends and manipulated me into hanging out with you? After you've embarrassed me in front of them? Why would I like a guy who had to contrive a situation like this just to get me to spend ten minutes with him? You're a chicken."

Robin leaned back in his chair and looked her in the eye. "And why would I like a girl who wasn't strong enough to tell Dirk her feelings? You're as big a chicken as I am."

Then he smiled and raised an eyebrow. "You participated in this setup, too. You just thought the outcome would be different."

"So don't like me. I don't care."

She grabbed her bag and stood to go. Robin rose and took her by the arm. "Well, I *do* like you."

"Why? Because I'm pretty? Because I'm tall and thin? Because I dress like the women you dream about? You don't know anything about me."

"And what do you know about Dirk?"

"I know that I like him."

Robin laughed. "No. You know that he's good-looking, that he's a star athlete, and that's he's the most popular guy at camp. Did you also know that he's a messy pig? That he can't spell my last name? That he listens to horrible hippie music and is a sore loser?"

Sabrina started for the door. "You can't *talk* me into liking you. That's not how it works."

"And you could never talk Dirk into liking you. He likes Lucy. He's liked her since the first day of camp. So what's the point in being angry about something you can't change?"

Sabrina stopped at the doorway. She turned around and looked at Robin. "I'll tell you what the point is: Lucy Camden is the first real friend I've made at this camp. And she hurt me." Sabrina's voice began to shake. "This has nothing to do with Dirk. And it certainly has nothing to do with you."

She opened the door and slammed it behind her.

Which is when she spotted Lucy and Dirk beneath the window, cowering behind the jade bushes.

Lucy stood up. But before she could say, "This is all my fault," Sabrina's hand was already in the air, stopping her words.

"You're a fake, Lucy Camden."

And with that, she turned around and ran off down the trail.

Ten minutes later, Lucy entered the cabin. In the middle of the floor, between the two twin beds, was a line of electrical tape dividing the room into two sections.

Sabrina lay in bed, her back to Lucy. The message was loud and clear: the tape was meant to serve as a wall between them, and Sabrina didn't want Lucy to cross it.

Lucy rolled her eyes. "You can't be serious."

But Sabrina didn't say anything. Instead, she reached up for the night-light and turned it off. The room went pitch-black.

Lucy sighed and sat down on her own bed. Then she reached over and turned the light back on. "This is a fifth-grade antic, Sabrina."

Sabrina pulled her cover up over her ears and eyes.

Lucy took a deep breath. *I'm not going to react to this childish behavior.*

Then she talked to the lump beneath the blanket. "I don't know how you deal with conflict in your family, but in mine, we talk about it. Like adults."

Sabrina yanked off the blanket and scoffed. "The whole reason we're in this situation is because you were afraid to deal with the fact that you and Dirk liked one another. Instead of talking to me about it, you enlisted me in a stupid game."

Lucy was as surprised by the severity of Sabrina's words as Robin had been. She was right. The game Lucy and Dirk had played with her was no less childish than the strip of tape Sabrina had placed across the floor.

"You're right," said Lucy.

"I know I am. And I know that you're basically a nice person, and that you're going to admit all your wrongdoing and apologize for it, and I'm still going to feel like a fool."

Lucy stepped across the line of tape and sat on Sabrina's bed. "I'm the one who should feel like a fool."

"But you don't. You feel guilty, and there's a difference. I'm the one everyone feels sorry for, and there's nothing I hate more than being pitied. I feel like every-body's laughing at me."

Lucy shook her head. "Robin feels like a jerk. I *am* a jerk. And Dirk's kicking him-self for being so stupid. You look like the *hero* in all this."

Sabrina lay there in silence, soaking up Lucy's words. When she finally sat up, Lucy saw that Sabrina's face was tearstained. Sabrina immediately pulled her legs up under her and scooted back against the bed's headboard.

"When I was nine years old, I came home from school and my mother was sitting on the kitchen floor, with pictures of my dad all around her, crying. She wouldn't tell us what was wrong, but my dad wasn't in the house. The next morning, she packed up all the pictures and all the gifts he'd ever given us, and took them to Goodwill. After that, she never spoke his name again and never told us what happened."

Lucy looked at Sabrina, concerned. "Did he die?"

Sabrina shook her head. "He cheated on her with her best friend. And we've still never talked about it. *That's* how my family deals with conflict. We close the door and we don't open it again."

Lucy reached out and took Sabrina's hand. "Well, I'm opening it for you. So talk to me."

Sabrina's eyes teared up. "I trusted you. And since my dad left, I don't trust very many people."

"I'm sorry—"

Sabrina cut her off. "Let me finish. I've liked Dirk for three years, and you're the only person I've ever told. So I feel really betrayed, Lucy."

Lucy nodded. "You should. I'm guilty of everything you've blamed me for. I should have just told you straight up that I liked Dirk. It was disrespectful and it assumed that you weren't adult enough to handle the situation. Instead, I tried to avoid the consequences of my own choices by trying to trick you into falling for some-one else."

Sabrina started to thank Lucy for the apology, but this time it was Lucy who cut in on Sabrina.

"I want you to know that your friend-ship is worth more to me than a weeklong romance with a guy I might never see again. I'll break it off with Dirk if that will prove that my friendship and my sorrow are real."

Sabrina shook her head. "Just be straight up with me, Lucy. I want a friend I can count on."

Lucy stuck out her hand to shake. "You've got one."

The two girls hugged, and then Lucy shook her finger at Sabrina. "And by the way—I think you should reconsider your stance on Robin. That boy is a *hottie*!"

Sabrina raised an eyebrow. "Okay, okay. He *was* getting cuter as the night went on. Especially when he started arguing with me. He's sharp, I'll give him that."

Lucy grinned. "You weren't so shabby yourself. You nailed him on a few points."

Sabrina grinned. "I did, didn't I?"

Lucy nodded, and took Sabrina's palm. She turned it over and pretended to read the lines. "I foresee a passionate future if you'd give it a chance."

Sabrina shrugged. "Whatever. Boys are like baseballs. They gotta be out of the park to get my attention."

Lucy laughed and held up her hand for Sabrina's high five. Then Sabrina started to laugh. "You should have seen your face when I caught you hiding in those bushes. I wish I'd had a camera!"

Mrs. Camden was jumping up and down in Simon's office, delighted by the news he had given her: two of her three stocks had spiked, and she made sixty-six dollars!

"Don't pull the money out now," she advised him. "Let's keep the stocks so we can keep making money."

Simon shook his head. "I don't advise it, Mom. Everyone will be selling their shares, and the stock prices will plunge. You'll lose money instead of making it."

Mrs. Camden's joy turned to concern. So far, Simon had been right. "So what do you advise?"

Simon turned to his computer and typed in a ticker code. A company name popped up on the screen. "This is a bio company that I just got a hot tip on. Let's put the sixty-six dollars there."

Mrs. Camden nodded. "Perfect! Except I think you should put *all* the money there. The three hundred dollars, too."

Simon hit a few more keys on his computer and a graph popped up. The graph,

which was shaped like a pie, was titled
Mom's Money. A small blue sliver read
Profit, and the rest of the pie, which was
pink, read *Initial Investment*. Simon
pointed to the small blue sliver.

"That's your profit, Mom. Your sixty-six
dollars. We agreed to reinvest only that. The
pink part of the pie is your initial investment. We agreed to put that back in your
savings account, where it's safe. I advise that
we stick to this plan. It's risk-free."

Mrs. Camden stared at the pie, her
thoughts turning fast in her mind. She
really liked the excitement of playing the
stock market. What could it hurt to invest
everything? After all, what was three hundred dollars in the 21st century?

"Any other options?" she asked.

Simon nodded. "I can invest everything, if that's what you want. But I have to
charge a fifteen-dollar brokerage fee for
going against my advice."

Mrs. Camden didn't have a problem
with that. She had saved fifteen dollars at
the grocery store using coupons just this
morning. But even more important, she
was feeling lucky. "Charge away!" she
cried.

NINE

The next afternoon, Lucy was wrapping up her carpentry class, pleased that her students had already completed the framework of a clubhouse. So far, she'd been surprised by her students' overwhelming enthusiasm. It made the time go by quickly.

"Everybody put your tools in your belts, and hang the belts on your assigned hooks. That's it for the day."

A grumble was heard among the kids—they weren't ready to go. They wanted to complete the clubhouse so they could start painting it.

Lucy smiled. "We still have three days to finish. Don't worry. It will look fabulous."

A short-haired girl raised her hand. "But what will we do with it when we're done?"

"We're donating it to the camp. Then if you come back next year, you can use it," Lucy said.

A boy in the back raised his hand, and Lucy nodded to him. "Yes, Jackson?"

The boy seemed nervous. He was a quiet kid, who didn't normally talk. "Um, Ms. Lucy, I was just wondering why you like to build things so much."

Lucy knew the answer before he even finished the question. "The most important thing a person can do is to help another person in need. Some people need simple things, like food or water, or even friends. And we can all help people who need those things, right?"

The kids all nodded voraciously. Lucy continued. "But there are people who need homes, too, and that's a more difficult problem to solve, but a very common problem in this country. So I like building things because it helps solve a significant problem—the housing crisis. I like building homes for people who need them."

Just then, Lucy saw Dirk standing in

the doorway of the classroom. He was listening to her, and had been for a while. He smiled as she finished addressing her class.

"Everyone's excused. See you tomorrow!"

The class filed out of the room as Dirk entered. "You're very passionate about this, aren't you?"

Lucy smiled. "How can you tell?"

Dirk put his arm through hers and looked at his watch. "Oh, you only ran . . . a half hour late."

The two walked in silence across the quad, and finally, Dirk turned to her. His face was serious. "So you know that question your little sister asked?"

Lucy nodded, and gently placed her hand over his mouth again. "Like I said, you don't have to answer that."

Dirk tenderly peeled her fingers away. "What if I want to answer it?"

Lucy took a deep breath. Dirk could immediately tell that something was wrong.

"What is it?"

"I'm really bothered by what we did to Sabrina."

"So am I."

Lucy looked at him. "Are you?"

Dirk nodded. "Yes and no. I think our intentions were right, so I don't think we can beat ourselves up anymore for not having the insight to handle the situation better. But am I bothered by the fact that we hurt her? Yes. Very much so. But I also know that we've each apologized to her, and if she can't accept that, then it becomes her issue, not ours."

Lucy knew he was right, and also knew that Sabrina *had* accepted the apology. But for some reason, she still sighed. "That's such a guy response."

Dirk's brow furrowed. "What does that mean?"

"It's just so logical."

"And what's wrong with that?"

Lucy shrugged again. "Nothing."

Dirk looked at her. "I don't think this is about Sabrina, is it?"

Lucy leaned up and kissed Dirk's cheek. "I'm not sure what it's about. I just have a lot on my mind. I'm sorry."

Dirk tried to read into Lucy's gaze but couldn't. The certainty that had been there before was gone. He put his hands in his pockets.

"So back to the question your sister asked . . ."

Two hours later, Lucy was standing in the camp's central cabin. It was the only cabin with a pay phone. She dialed a telephone number and waited.

Seconds later, she heard the familiar voice of her mother, which comforted her. After talking to Dirk about their relationship, she had felt confused and unsettled.

"So how's camp?" Mrs. Camden asked.

"It's great," Lucy enthused. "My class is amazing, all the kids really dig carpentry, and these two boys agreed to sign up for their local Habitat chapters. Oh, and guess what else? Our clubhouse is almost built."

There was a short pause on the other end, as though Mrs. Camden were waiting to hear something else. "But . . . ?" she asked expectantly.

Lucy laughed, "But nothing."

Mrs. Camden pounced on Lucy's hesitancy, sensing that something was wrong. "*But* there hasn't been a single mention of a guy, and your voice sounds flat."

"Flat?" Lucy asked, deadpan.

"That's right. Flat."

Lucy couldn't help but smile to herself. Her mother knew her *way* too well. "His name is Dirk," she said.

"And you still haven't answered my *But . . .* ?" Mrs. Camden demanded.

"Because there are so many."

"So start with the biggest one."

Lucy explained the whole situation with Sabrina, embarrassed to admit her part in the previous night's shenanigans.

But the more she talked about it, the more Mrs. Camden assured Lucy that even though the setup was deceptive, she had handled the aftermath well—by accepting responsibility for it, and by apologizing to Sabrina. And the more assured Lucy became about it, the more certain she was that Sabrina was not the cause of her angst about Dirk.

Mrs. Camden sensed this, too. "So on to the other *But . . .* ?"

Lucy took a deep breath, and finally said what had been on her mind all day. "But camp's over in three days," she moaned.

Mrs. Camden laughed. "Oh, Lucy!

You're so young and you have so much life ahead of you."

Lucy's moan was followed by a groan. "I know! That's why I'm trying not to get too attached or excited. I mean, we're both going off to college. How do you make a long-distance relationship work? Do you e-mail for four years? Hitchhike cross-country between classes—"

Mrs. Camden interrupted her. "My point is that you've got the time to get excited, and to get attached to things that might never work out."

Lucy sighed. "Are you saying it won't work out?"

"I'm saying enjoy your freedom before you have bills to pay, careers to worry about, taxes to write off, mouths to feed, health insurance to find, retirement plans to consider, stock portfolios to—"

Lucy gasped. "Okay, okay! I get your point! I'll relax and enjoy what I've got, all right?"

But Mrs. Camden wasn't finished with her sermon. "I had more fun at your age than I ever had at any other time in my life—"

"Mom," Lucy pleaded. "I hear you."

"Good," Mrs. Camden stated.

"And by the way," Lucy added. "What I've got is *incredible*. This guy is smart, gorgeous, witty, sweet, compassionate, interesting, charming, mischievous—"

Now it was her mother's turn to moan. "Okay, okay! I get the point!"

Lucy smiled again. "But enough about me. How about you?"

Mrs. Camden's voice turned jovial as she whispered, "Your dad thinks he's being very sneaky. . . ."

Up the stairs from Mrs. Camden, her husband entered Simon's office and quietly closed the door. He sat down on Lucy's bed and looked somberly at Simon. "Tell me the truth. Who's winning?"

Simon sighed as he spun slowly around in his desk chair. "For the record, I'm annoyed that you and Mom have turned my business into a hockey arena."

Reverend Camden leaned over and patted his son on the back. "Thanks for yet another lesson, son, but for your knowledge—we're having a blast."

"Well, I'm not. So pay up if you want

info." Simon held out his hand.

Reverend Camden threw his hands into the air. "I'm your dad!" he shouted.

"And you're losing money!" Simon retorted.

His father's jaw dropped, horrified. "I'm losing?"

Simon calmly nodded. "I told you not to invest in TimeStar."

Reverend Camden collapsed on the bed, staring slack-jawed at the wall. "How's your mom doing?" he asked.

Simon held out his palm. The reverend sighed, then pulled out the money and put it in his son's hand. Simon opened his wallet. "She's doubled her money in three days."

Reverend Camden grabbed Lucy's pillow and covered his face with it. He groaned for a minute, mumbling something about "six hundred dollars," then finally regained his composure. He sat up, nodding soberly. "Then put my money wherever she's putting hers."

Simon sighed. "I don't recommend it."

"Why?" his father asked.

"Because her company just lost its president, who cashed in all his stock—a good indication that he believes the company has no future."

Reverend Camden nodded. "Then put it where yours is."

"I suggest splitting it between stocks, like I did originally with Mom," Simon counseled.

Reverend Camden shook his head. "No. Put it where yours is."

Simon shrugged. "Fine. But it'll cost you."

TEN

Early the next morning on Wednesday, before the other campers woke, Ruthie and Bailey sneaked off to the horse stables. Yesterday, Ruthie had seen one of the older kids riding a beautiful thoroughbred through the woods.

"It's not fair that they won't let our age group ride," Ruthie complained to her new best friend. "I've taken lessons before."

Bailey looked at Ruthie, impressed. "I've never even petted a horse," Bailey said. "We've always lived in the city, so there aren't any horses."

Ruthie and Bailey passed the tack shed, and Ruthie explained its purpose. "That's where you keep your equipment."

"Equipment?"

Ruthie nodded. "Like wire brushes to brush the horse's mane, and tools to clean dirt and stuff out of its hooves. You have to tack your horse every time before you ride."

She pointed to a row of riding helmets and saddles in the tack shed. "If we got to ride, this is where we'd get our hats and saddles, too."

Bailey noticed that there were two different kinds of saddles. "What's the difference?" she asked.

"The big one," Ruthie explained, "is for Western-style riding. That's what cowboys ride on. It's easier to stay inside of, so you won't fall off if the horse bucks. Those little ones are for English riding."

"English?" Bailey asked.

Ruthie nodded. "You know on TV where you see the riders wearing hats and jodhpurs—those tight white pants with the big tall boots over them?"

Bailey laughed. "Yeah! Where they jump over those hurdle things?"

"Yeah," Ruthie confirmed. "Well, that's English riding. And that's what those little saddles are for."

Just then, Ruthie let out an excited whoop. She had just spotted the thorough-bred she had seen yesterday. She ran through the stables toward it, then shouted out the name written on its nameplate. "Kentucky!" she bellowed, greeting it with warmth. "You're a beauty!"

But before she could reach in and stroke its long, tight jowls, a deep voice called out behind her, "No kids in the stables."

She and Bailey turned to discover Mrs. Stout standing in the doorway. She was draped in a fuzzy orange robe. Bailey stamped her foot. "That's not what the sign says!"

"Yeah," Ruthie agreed. She read the words on the sign that was posted near the entrance. "It just says to not feed the animals."

Mrs. Stout pulled the robe tighter around her and tied the cotton belt into a double knot. Clearly, she had just crawled out of bed. "It's what *I* say. My cabin is next to the stables, and I don't like the noise."

Bailey huffed and Ruthie sighed, but Mrs. Stout didn't budge. The two girls finally spun around and left.

As Ruthie and Bailey left the stables, they heard a *Psssttt!* come from an empty stall. Ruthie turned around and saw the blond boy sitting on the iron fence, his legs dangling through the bars.

Ruthie turned to Bailey and mouthed, "That's the kid I told you about."

He motioned her over, and she marched straight up to him. "Why have you been pulling my curls?" she demanded.

He leaned his head through the bars. "Because I like you."

Ruthie rolled her eyes. "Well, I like you, too."

The boy, whose name was Tanner, reached out and pulled the first curl he could wrap his fingers around. Ruthie sighed, then reached up through the bars and pulled on his short blond bangs. "So what do you want?" Ruthie asked.

He looked down the center aisle between the stalls, to make sure Mrs. Stout was gone. "I can help you ride the horses," he whispered.

A few hours later, in the camp cafeteria, a very unexpected event took place. It started when Tara walked past Sabrina, who was sitting alone at a cafeteria table. As expected, Tara pushed her nose up in the air, causing her gang of friends to burst out laughing as they strutted by.

A few tables down, Robin, who was also sitting alone, shouted Tara's name. Tara turned around and grinned—thinking he dug her joke. "What's up?"

Robin raised an eyebrow. "I wouldn't pick a fight with Sabrina if I were you."

Tara, surprised, started to retort when Sabrina glared at Robin from across the room. "I don't need you to stand up for me, Robin."

Tara spun around, covered her mouth in mock shock, and looked at Sabrina. "My *goodness*! Princess Van Raming has actually spoken. To what do we owe the occasion?"

But Sabrina said nothing, and returned to eating.

Tara scoffed at her silence. "Cat got your tongue—or are you just too dumb to talk?"

Robin stood up and grinned. "Sabrina doesn't waste her wit on dolts."

"Wit?" Tara mused. "I didn't realize she

knew more than ten words."

Robin shrugged. "If you were a bit more interesting, perhaps she'd take the time to respond."

Tara laughed. "Are you saying our own little Barbie has brains?"

Robin cocked his hip out and struck an exaggerated magazine pose. "Not to mention style. Check her out. She's so demure, so sophisticated, so absolutely unconcerned with your taunting."

Sabrina couldn't help herself: she cracked a smile. Then she decided to play along. She stood up—all five feet ten inches of her—crossed her arms, put a spiked heel on the cafeteria seat, and raised an eyebrow like a femme fatale.

"Like I said, Robin," she cooed. "I don't need you to fight my fights."

Robin smiled at Tara and raised his hands. "You see? She only expends her energy on the people who matter."

Annoyed that Robin had indeed pegged the situation—in all these years, Sabrina had never once reacted to Tara's antics—Tara had a desperate idea.

She picked up a spoonful of mashed

potatoes. "Let's see how she reacts to a food fight."

Tara aimed her spoon right at Sabrina's pink suede pants. She hurled the fluffy chunks and they landed with a *kersplat*, right on Sabrina's left thigh.

A collective gasp went up in the camp cafeteria.

But Sabrina didn't flinch. Instead, she calmly reached down to her cafeteria tray and grabbed a slab of turkey. She smiled and . . .

Zoom!

The turkey plastered itself across *Robin's* forehead.

Tara was livid. Sabrina had ignored her again! Tara grabbed a handful of peas and in a fury of anger blasted them at Sabrina. The little green pellets splattered across Sabrina's black vinyl tube top.

Sabrina glanced down at herself. She was covered in little mashed green beads. Suddenly, she burst out laughing. She laughed harder than she had ever laughed in her life. It was funny!

Then she calmly grabbed her mashed potatoes and walked straight across the cafeteria, her heels *click-click-clacking* across the linoleum.

She stopped right in front of Robin. She looked at his pretty, smooth, golden skin. And then she smeared the potatoes across his entire face.

He smiled, reached down into his cafeteria tray, and smeared his potatoes across her face.

Then they kissed.

And that's when the whole place *really* went berserk.

Back on Cyber Street, Simon decided to take a lunch break. He stood up, stretched, and pushed his chair neatly in beneath his desk. Then he filed his many stock market reports, company profiles, and prospectuses in their respective folders.

He took a step back and looked at the desk. It was uncluttered, fastidious, and the information was easily accessible. Simon liked order. The thing he liked least in the world was the unexpected—unless it was the unexpected twists and turns of Wall Street.

He smiled, walked out of the office, then hopped down the first set of stairs to his parents' and siblings' hallway. All was quiet in the Camden house. For once.

Simon ambled down the second set of stairs and entered the kitchen. He opened the refrigerator and was excited to find it stocked full of tasty items. It was a good day.

Upstairs, Matt peeked into Simon's office and was delighted to find it empty. Even better was the fact that Simon had left his computer on, and the screen was filled by a stock-trading company's Web site.

Matt leaned over and quickly typed in a ticker code. A price appeared next to the number: *$147.25.*

Then Matt typed in a few more words. The words *Investment: Zero* appeared.

Suddenly, he heard footsteps behind him. Before he could exit the screen, Simon entered the room.

"Get out!" Simon shouted. "Go do something with the guys, and leave me to my work!"

But Matt wasn't deterred. Instead, he crossed his arms combatively and stared at Simon. "I paid you a fee to buy my stock, and you still haven't bought it."

Exasperated, Simon yelled, "Because I can get it for cheaper at closing!"

Matt laughed. "You don't know that. It's just a guess. It's a gamble, like everything else. You may be able to convince Mom and Dad that you're so technologically superior that it makes you a stock market expert, but you can't convince me. I'm onto your game, Simon."

Simon yanked out his desk chair and sat down. He began furiously typing in ticker codes. "Fine. I'll buy your stock for one-forty-seven and a quarter. That'll give you a whole two shares. And when they announce their company layoffs this afternoon, and those two shares are worth nothing, I won't say *I told you so*."

Matt smiled and leaned in over Simon's shoulder. "So how are Mom and Dad doing?"

Simon kept typing with one hand and held his palm out with the other.

ELEVEN

Ruthie's fish, Skipper, had gotten smelly after four days. *Really* smelly. But she had kept it for a reason: she knew she'd eventually need it for something. The something had finally come.

It was past midnight, and she and Tanner were standing quietly outside Mrs. Stout's cabin. Inside, all of her lights were out. She was certainly asleep by now. Around them, a late-night calm had settled throughout the camp.

Tanner opened the fish's mouth, and Ruthie reached inside with her fishing pole hook. She felt around for a small hole, and then reattached the hook to the roof of the fish's mouth.

Tanner turned on his flashlight and pointed it upward into the trees. Way up at the very top of a sycamore tree, two large branches forked in different directions. The belly of the fork had formed a cradle, and a long, fuzzy, black-and-white-ringed tail wrapped around the cradle's circular edge. Tanner was shining the light on a sleeping raccoon. He looked at Ruthie and nodded.

Ruthie wound the string of her fishing pole up tight, the fish still dangling from the end. Then she tossed the pole over her shoulder, looked up at the raccoon, and cast the line—fish and all—up at the tree.

Just below the raccoon's tail, the fish flopped against the bark of the tree. The noise was loud enough to wake the sleeping creature. Tanner turned off his flashlight as the fish tumbled back toward the ground. The curious raccoon peeked out of its nest, then hopped down the tree after the fish.

Delighted at their good luck, Tanner and Ruthie began quietly backing up in the direction of Mrs. Stout's cabin, pulling the fish along after them. The raccoon followed.

Once Ruthie reached the front porch, Tanner stopped her from backing into the front door. He pointed toward an open bedroom window, and Ruthie grabbed the fish off the hook and flung it inside.

As the raccoon hopped through the window after it, the two kids fled into the stable. They crouched beside the front door and watched Mrs. Stout's cabin.

First, there was a scream. Next, a bedside light went on. Then the raccoon, fish in mouth, leaped out of the window and raced off into the woods.

Mrs. Stout, frazzled and angry in her orange robe, which she had thrown on backward, flung the door open and ran off after the terrified creature.

As soon as she disappeared into the forest, Tanner ran toward Kentucky's stable, and Ruthie grabbed a Western saddle out of the tack shed.

Moments later, the two crawled up on the fence, threw the saddle on, and dived toward the horse. They landed perfectly on the horse's back, snug on the leather saddle. Ruthie reached under the horse's belly and cinched up the girth.

Tanner reached out and opened the

latch on the gate. He pulled it open, and the horse bolted out like a quarter horse at the races.

Before they even reached the stable exit, the horse started bucking. Ruthie turned around and looked back at the gate. Her eyes opened wide in surprise when she read the nameplate. They weren't on Kentucky at all—they were riding Thunder, the rowdiest horse in the entire camp!

Far up in the hills, Lucy was doing some sneaking around of her own. She knocked lightly on Dirk's window, and in seconds, he was standing outside before her.

Dirk noticed the anxious look on her face, and his own face paled. "What's wrong?" he asked.

Lucy wrung her hands together, unsure if she was doing the right thing. "I've been doing some thinking," she began. Then she sighed. *Doing some thinking is an understatement. I've been up all night, worrying, obsessing. . . .*

"About what?" asked Dirk.

Lucy took a breath and centered herself. "I heard about Robin and Sabrina kissing in the cafeteria . . . but that doesn't mean I should ignore her feelings and jump into something with you. And what's the use anyway? We're both going off to college in different states, and—"

Dirk jumped in before she could finish her sentence. "Stop. Just stop. There's no time like the present, I always say."

"What do you mean?" asked Lucy.

In answer, Dirk leaned over, put his arms around her waist, and flipped her up over his shoulder. Lucy stifled a yelp as he ran off with her in the moonlight.

Four hundred yards west, just off the camp's backmost trail, Ruthie had convinced Tanner to let her crawl up front in order to take the reins. After all, they were practically lost, and the horse was in complete control of the journey. Tanner's horsemanship was far from impressive.

Now Ruthie had the reins and she was battling the willpower of a horse that was barely broken. Even worse, they were headed for the edge of a cliff up ahead, which dropped off a hundred feet. Ruthie knew that if the horse continued running, the sharp crest would spook the horse— and then they'd really be in trouble. She had to turn the horse around.

She grabbed the reins tightly, then yanked hard to the right. At the same moment, she dug her right heel into the horse's side.

Shocked by the determination and confidence of its new master, the horse spun around to the right, doing a 180-degree turn. They were now pointing in exactly the direction Ruthie wanted.

"Now *halt*," she ordered, pulling straight back, careful to exert equal pressure on both reins, and lifting her heel from the horse's belly. The horse froze.

Ruthie breathed a sigh of relief, then leaned forward. She reached out and stroked the horse's neck. "It's okay," she cooed, aware of fear in the horse's eyes. "We're afraid of you, and you're afraid of us," she said. "Isn't that silly?"

Ruthie's words calmed the horse down, and it began to nestle its head up into her gentle hand.

"Wow," Tanner said. "You really know how to ride. We could have been dead."

Ruthie nodded. "One wrong step over that crest, and *splat*!"

Tanner laughed, then pointed westward. "Look at what's down there," he said.

Ruthie looked behind them, where Tanner was pointing, and her mouth dropped open. She had been so busy trying to control the horse that she hadn't even noticed that the ocean was right below them!

Tanner pulled gently on one of Ruthie's curls, as if to ask her a question. Ruthie looked back at him. "Can I hold your hand?" he asked.

Ruthie shrugged. "I've never held a boy's hand before. But sure. Why not?"

Tanner reached around her waist and placed his hand on top of hers. The two sat there together, in silence, looking out at the ocean. Ruthie looked down at Tanner's hand and grinned. It actually felt good!

TWELVE

After a careful run down a steep trail, Dirk gently dropped Lucy feetfirst into a soft sand dune. For the first time since he had picked her up, she had the chance to look around. And what she saw delighted her.

They were feet away from a low, approaching wave. Lucy shouted and ran toward it, yanking off her shoes as she went. The cool sand felt great between her toes. She collided midthigh with the gentle wave, and was happily surprised by the warmth of the Pacific water.

She turned around and spotted Dirk. He was standing with a big smile on his face, watching her attack the wave that most girls would run from.

"Come on!" Lucy yelled.

As if a whistle had blown to signal the beginning of a race, Dirk was off and running toward Lucy. She squealed when she saw the look in his eyes: he was going to tackle her!

Lucy braced herself, digging both feet into the sinking sand, hoping it would give her additional balance. She held her arms up in front of her, like a Kenpo karate master.

"You're going down!" Dirk shouted.

Lucy laughed. "You're going down with me!"

He leaped at her with the zeal of a puppy, and the two tumbled into the waves. The warm water felt wonderful.

Lucy shaved a handful of sea foam off the water and smeared it onto Dirk's chin. "So this is how you'll look when you're old and gray."

Dirk grabbed his own sea foam and lathered it onto Lucy's chin. "You'll still be beautiful."

Then Lucy's foot hit something on the seafloor. "Ouch."

"What's wrong?"

Lucy bent down and felt around in the

sand. Maybe it had just been driftwood or a clamshell. Whatever it was, she couldn't find it. She shrugged. "I think I stepped on a shell."

Then Dirk's eyes widened as he felt the object with his own foot. He smiled as he reached down. "I know what it is."

He retrieved an empty glass bottle and held it up. "Well, look what we have here!" he declared with an air of mystery.

Lucy looked at the bottle, unimpressed. "A glass bottle," she stated.

"Not just any bottle," Dirk warned, shaking his finger. "A very special bottle."

Lucy crossed her arms. "Special?"

Dirk touched her nose like he was wiping chocolate from it. "That's right. Special."

Then he put his forefinger inside the bottle, as if to retrieve something. He pretended to pull out a piece of paper, and then mimed opening the imaginary slip. Lucy laughed when she realized what he was doing. He was pretending to find a message in a bottle.

"My reading glasses, please?" Dirk held out his hand and Lucy pretended to put his reading glasses in it.

Dirk put them on, and his eyes went to the imaginary paper, perusing the unwritten words. Then he read them aloud to Lucy. "'You are talented beyond words, intelligent beyond understanding, and beautiful beyond comprehension. You will travel far, meet great people, affect many lives, and the world will be better for it.'"

Unexpectedly, Lucy's eyes filled with tears.

"Hey now!" Dirk protested. "That should make you laugh. That should make you happy."

"I am happy," Lucy sniffed, trying to stop new tears from forming. But she couldn't help it. It was all too perfect—the romantic night, the guy before her, the future that awaited—for her to just stand there and feel nothing. She felt everything. Joy, fear, anticipation, sorrow . . .

Dirk took her hand in his and led her up toward the beach. When they reached the sand dune, he sat and pulled her down next to him.

"Now tell me what's wrong," he said.

Lucy wiped away her tears and smiled. "Have you ever felt like you're at a place in your life where a hundred roads have come together? Like you're standing at the center of a wheel and a thousand spokes are reaching toward you, and every spoke represents a wonderful choice that you have to make?"

Dirk nodded. "I feel that way right now. I've got a soccer scholarship to one school and a science scholarship to another. But my mom wants me to go to our community college so I can watch my little sister grow up. And then there's this great girl that I just met. Maybe you know her? Her name's Lucy?"

Lucy smiled and then collapsed on her back with a groan. "I know her! And she feels exactly the same way—excited, confused, devastated."

Dirk looked at her. "I have a rule in life that I live by. You want to hear it?"

Lucy nodded.

"Whenever I have more reasons to say no than to say yes, then that's when I say yes. Because that's risking, and risk is what allows us to learn and to grow. And growth is what allows us to know ourselves."

Lucy stared at Dirk in wonder. How had she stumbled across such an amazing guy?

Lucy reached up and touched Dirk's face. "When I first met you, I fell for your looks," she admitted. "And then I fell for your sense of humor. You make me laugh, Dirk."

Dirk smiled as Lucy continued. "But now I've fallen for something deeper. I don't know what the future holds, but I do know this: what we have is real, and it's worth jumping into, right now."

Lucy touched her lips to his as Dirk enfolded her in his arms. The kiss was long and tender, and Lucy wanted it to last forever.

Instead, it was abruptly interrupted by the sudden thunder of hooves. Yards away, Ruthie and Tanner were racing down the beach like cowboys in pursuit of a wild stallion, unaware of Lucy and Dirk. Lucy moaned when she heard her little sister's bellowing squall, which was followed by a boy's wild holler.

Unsure of whether to hide or to bust Ruthie for horse-thievery, Lucy cringed as she announced to Dirk, "That's my sister."

Ruthie froze the instant she heard Lucy's voice carry across the wind. She yanked hard on her right rein.

The horse turned on a dime, then stopped abruptly. Delighted by her horse's fine behavior, Ruthie stroked its mane as she looked down at the busted twosome before her.

Lucy jumped up, her hands immediately going to her hips. "What are you doing here?" she demanded in her best big-sister voice.

Ruthie raised a mischievous eyebrow. "I could ask you the same thing."

But before Lucy could defend herself, a giant spotlight spilled down from the crest above—and the four were illuminated as clearly as actors on a stage.

"What's going on?" Lucy asked Dirk, dumbfounded. She put her hand over her eyes, then squinted up at the giant light on the hill.

Dirk groaned, "Oh no . . ." He began to explain, but his words were cut off by the resounding voice of Mrs. Stout, who was shouting down at them with the electronic aid of a bullhorn.

"Lucy Camden, Dirk Porter, Ruthie Camden, and Tanner Goodman: report to my office immediately!"

THIRTEEN

Lucy, Ruthie, Dirk, and Tanner sat quietly in four chairs before Mrs. Stout, who was determined to bar them from attending future camps by making them sign an admission-of-guilt form. They had all refused.

On the office wall, a clock revealed that it was three in the morning. Lucy struggled to keep her eyes open, and Ruthie failed at suppressing a yawn.

Mrs. Stout smiled. Her new tactic was to wear them down by keeping them up as long as possible. She looked evenly at the group. "You woke me up with your shenanigans, so now you'll stay up until we've all agreed on an appropriate punishment."

Lucy tried to focus on the task at hand. "I just think that barring Dirk and me from ever teaching camp again is a bit harsh."

Mrs. Stout, as strong willed and clear thinking as if it were noontime, shook her head. "I disagree. You're here to set an example. And I'll continue to disagree until you all sign this paper."

Ruthie sighed. "Fine. I'll sign it."

But before Ruthie could grab the pen, Lucy found just enough energy to pinch Ruthie into stopping.

"Ouch!"

Lucy looked at her and shook her head. "If you sign that, you won't be allowed to earn a scholarship next year. Which means you won't have the money to come back. Ever."

Ruthie whined, "I don't care. I'm tired."

Tanner nodded. He was fading faster than a kid waiting up for Santa Claus. "Me too. I'll sign."

Lucy looked at Dirk, hoping for his persuasive assistance. But Dirk just shrugged. "I don't want to sign, but . . . I'm getting sleepy, too. I don't know how much more of a fight I can put up."

Mrs. Stout smiled and did a little tap dance to show them all how energetic she was. It was a very odd moment. "You know the great thing about getting old?" she asked. "You can stay up all night!"

Annoyed by the rising cacophonous sound of Mrs. Stout's clamoring taps, Lucy leaned over to Dirk. "Just hold out until the other sponsors are awake. We can reason with them—especially Mr. Sanchez. He's a powerful board member, and a big fan of mine. Once we sign those papers," she reminded him, "we're agreeing to never come back as teachers or counselors."

But Dirk's head was beginning to droop over his chest. "I don't think I can stay awake," he admitted.

Just then, Lucy had a great idea. "Then fall asleep right here," she said, her voice getting louder as she looked at Mrs. Stout. "We'll just sleep until the other sponsors come into the office."

Mrs. Stout smiled. "Go ahead," she chirped—and then tapped another irritating number on the tile floor. She was surprisingly good, but at this time in the morning, even a trumpet would have been preferable.

Ruthie and Tanner plugged their ears and stood up, fighting for the pen. After they'd both signed the paper, they hurried out as fast as their tired legs would take them.

Mrs. Stout looked at the remaining two, then climbed on top of the metal desk and began stomping. "I used to dance off-Broadway," she bragged. Her feet sounded like raining rocks on a cold tin roof. "And now I'm relegated to baby-sitting you little twerps!"

Dirk valiantly tried to sleep through the noise, but when Mrs. Stout began clapping chalkboard erasers together as she tapped, he caved. "Sorry, Luce, she's making me loony."

He leaned over, signed the sheet, and then slunk out of the office. Lucy glared up at her nemesis, determined to take the pain without complaint. "I'm not signing that paper."

Mrs. Stout shrugged, then raised the erasers over her head and began shouting "Hey!" with every stomp of her feet. A cloud of chalk dust swirled around her, and Lucy wryly noted that the only thing missing was a basket of fruit on the crazy lady's head.

"Fine!" Lucy shouted in desperation. "I'll sign it!" She picked up the pen, scribbled her name, and then marched out of the office.

Fifteen minutes later, Lucy trudged through her cabin door—eyes wild, hair mussed, clothes full of sand. She was surprised to find Sabrina awake.

Sabrina couldn't help but laugh. "Well, look what the cat dragged in!"

"Don't even go there," Lucy warned. Until she looked in the mirror. And then she had to laugh herself. "I look like I was in a hurricane!"

Sabrina's eyebrow went up. "From what we heard over the bullhorn, I bet that's not too far from the truth."

Lucy's jaw dropped. "You heard Mrs. Stout call us to her office?"

Sabrina nodded. "The whole camp did. Everyone's talking."

"But it's four in the morning! How is

that possible if nobody can leave their cabins?"

Sabrina waved her cell phone at Lucy, who collapsed on her bed.

"Outstanding. Not only have I been barred from teaching camp again, I'm now the subject of campwide gossip. I probably deserve it."

Sabrina shrugged. "Who cares? Did you have fun?"

Lucy nodded. "You're sure you're not upset with me for seeing Dirk?"

Sabrina laughed. "Upset? I'm elated. I owe so much to you!"

"You do?" Lucy asked.

"Robin is the most incredible guy. I don't know why I didn't see it before."

Lucy felt a small weight rise. "So you're really over Dirk?"

Sabrina's brow creased. "Dirk? Please. I couldn't even talk to the guy. I don't know what I was thinking. Robin is so perfect for me. He's really easy to talk to, he's got this wacky sense of humor, and we live less than ten miles apart. He's going to come visit my sister in the hospital."

"So tell me," Lucy said gently. "What's wrong with your sister?"

Sabrina sighed and explained that her sister had leukemia, a treatable but potentially deadly kind of recurring cancer. "Just when we think things are going great, it strikes again."

Lucy reached out and took her friend's hand. She squeezed it. "I'm sorry."

Sabrina shook her head. "Don't be. I'm just lucky that I can model. It's what pays all the bills. I've been modeling ever since we found out about her condition. Without it, I don't know what would happen to her."

Lucy shook her head. "I totally misjudged you, Sabrina. You're an *amazing* girl."

Sabrina thanked Lucy, then asked about her and Dirk. Lucy smiled proudly. "I've decided not to worry about it. Whatever happens, happens."

Sabrina hugged Lucy, then walked across the room where Lucy's boom box sat. She picked it up, spun around like a supermodel on a runway, and looked at Lucy with a raised eyebrow. "I went to all this trouble to convince Stout to give this back, and you haven't even played it?"

Lucy cringed. "Sorry."

Sabrina slipped her own CD inside,

and Lucy noticed the cover. It was rap!

Lucy laughed as Sabrina turned up the volume. *Mrs. Stout was right after all: I'm blaring rap in the middle of the night!*

Seconds later, there was a knock on the door and the girls from the next cabin, Tara and Monica, stepped inside. Tara smiled at Sabrina. "So you're hipper than I thought. And I'm a wad. Do you forgive me or what?"

Sabrina shrugged. "Well, since you're begging . . ."

Tara's jaw dropped. "Begging?"

And then she realized that Sabrina was playing her like a piano. She smiled. "Is that your music?"

Sabrina nodded, and Tara began to groove. "It's pretty phat," Tara admitted, then pointed outside as two more pajama-sporting guests arrived. "Anyone up for a street, er, uh, trail party?" she asked.

Two days later, after a long round of good-byes on the quad, Lucy and Ruthie grabbed their bags and headed off for their bus—where Dirk and Tanner were waiting.

Tanner looked at Ruthie and rolled his

eyes. "Mrs. Stout won't let me ride your bus. I have to get on the other one." Then he reached out and pulled a curl. "See you next year."

Ruthie pulled his bangs. "Yeah. See you next year."

Mrs. Stout leaned in. "Not on scholarship, you won't."

Ruthie huffed, then threw a look at Mrs. Stout. "You obviously don't know Ruthie Camden. I'll find enough money to come back," she loudly pronounced, then marched onto the bus.

Tanner ran up to the door. "I'll write!" he shouted.

Nearby, Lucy and Dirk hugged until the bus driver started honking. Then Dirk looked down at her. "We'll see each other again. That much I know."

Lucy nodded and wanted to say *I love you.* But she knew she had only known him for a week, and wanted to know him better. She'd save that for a day down the road, a day that was definitely right. "I can't wait," she said, then leaned up and kissed him quickly on the lips.

"Good-bye, Dirk."

Dirk shook his head—he didn't want to say good-bye. Instead, he held his hand up to his ear and mouth like a telephone. "I'll call you."

FOURTEEN

Saturday morning in the Camden living room was normally loud, but not this loud. Simon had called a family meeting, and now looked across the faces of his mother, father, and older brother.

"Due to a conflict of interest, I've decided not to broker any more deals for the three of you—as nobody will take my advice, which puts me in the unenviable position of watching your money go down the drain."

Simon stood up and opened his wallet as a flurry of protest went up. He produced nine crisp $100 bills, and handed three to each family member. "The fees I charged and my own substantial earnings have covered everybody's losses. Now take your initial investments and put them back in your lame savings accounts. Please."

Reverend Camden looked around the room, confused. His eyes came to rest on his wife. "You mean *everybody* lost?"

Mrs. Camden smiled sourly at him and he perked up a bit.

Simon nodded. "Everybody except the person who let me do my job."

Mr. and Mrs. Camden's eyes both shot to Matt. Matt shrugged and shook his head. "I didn't make any money," he said suspiciously, then looked back at his parents.

They shook their heads, then looked at each other. Mrs. Camden crossed her arms. "You actually made a profit, didn't you?"

The reverend shook his head. But his wife didn't believe him. "You little rat fink. You sneaked around all week, squeezing my tactics out of poor Simon, and then copying them. The only difference is that you pulled your money out last night instead of this morning."

The reverend laughed. "I wish that were the case, but Simon wouldn't tell me your tactics. I lost all right."

Confused, the three looked back at Simon, who smiled as the front door opened. Standing in the doorway was Mary. "Well, is someone going to help me with my bags, or what?"

Mrs. Camden joyfully shouted, "You're home!"

The reverend rushed over and grabbed her bags as Matt hugged her. "Welcome home, Mary!" Matt said. "What a surprise! How did you afford a ticket from Buffalo?"

Mary put her arm around Simon, who had managed her money all month. She'd bought the ticket with her profits. "I've got a hot tip for you guys."

"What?" Matt groaned.

Mary kissed Simon's forehead. "Not what, but who."

Mary turned to close the front door. But as soon as it shut, there was a loud yelp on the other side.

"Hey!"

Mary opened the door and found Lucy and Ruthie on the other side. Ruthie was holding her toe in pain. "Thanks a lot, Mary!"

Lucy threw her arms around her big sister. "What are you doing here?"

But before Mary could answer, Mrs. Camden put her arm on Lucy's shoulder. "How was camp?"

Lucy sighed. "It's a long story."

"I lost my camp scholarship!" Ruthie proudly announced. "Which means that next year, I have to *pay*. Anyone know how to make some quick dough?"

The whole family groaned as the telephone rang in the kitchen. All five kids took off running. But Lucy was the quickest and beat all of her siblings' reaching hands.

"Hello!" she said, running into her dad's study for privacy. But it wasn't Dirk. It was Sabrina, who was speaking a mile a minute.

"You'll never believe this. There were so many complaints about Stout and all her ridiculous rules that the camp board asked her to not come back next year—unless it's to teach tap! Not only that, your construction class was so popular that the kids raved to their parents, and Mr. Sanchez convinced the board to throw out all of Stout's complaints. They want you back, Lucy!"

When Lucy hung up the phone, she

ran into the living room and delivered a full report to Ruthie. "Guess what, Ruthie?" she said. "You're back up for the scholarship! Keep your grades high, and you're in!"

That night, Lucy was happy to have Mary back in the bedroom they had shared for so many years. The two girls stayed up talking until the wee hours.

As Mary drifted off to sleep, Lucy still felt like she had enough energy to light the entire world. Even though Dirk hadn't called, she wasn't worried or even upset. She *knew* he'd call. And even if he didn't, everything they shared was real, and every moment they had taught her something about herself and about life. Next week, she was leaving for college. She was ready.

Lucy looked out her window and simply whispered, "Thank you."

DON'T MISS THIS BRAND-NEW, HEARTWARMING COLLECTION OF ORIGINAL 7TH HEAVEN STORIES!

LUCY'S ANGEL

While visiting her grandfather in Arizona, Lucy Camden uncovers a beautiful angel ornament in his basement—one that her mother had cherished as a little girl but thought was lost forever. Now Lucy can't wait to get home to present the angel to Mrs. Camden! But as Lucy and Simon drive back to California, they encounter an expectant woman badly in need of help. Should they stop to help her? Or mind their own business so they can make it home in time for the church's big holiday party?

MARY'S GIFT

Flying home from Buffalo proves disastrous for Mary. During a layover in the Midwest, an unexpected blizzard forces her to camp out on the floor of an airport terminal along with hundreds of other furious travelers. Stuck in the middle of nowhere with strangers on Christmas Eve, Mary is stunned when one child's tears lead her to give a gift that gives her much more in return. . . .

MATT AND THE KING

Matt can't pass up the chance for a swingin' new year when Robbie invites him to a hotel/casino in Las Vegas. On their way, they pick up a stranded motorist. The man looks like Elvis, acts like Elvis, and sounds like Elvis! Has their New Year's celebration turned into a brush with a rock-'n'-roll angel?

Coming October 2001!
0-375-81419-1

LUCY'S
ANGEL

DON'T MISS THIS BRAND-NEW, ORIGINAL 7ᵀᴴ HEAVEN STORY

Now Available!

LEARNING THE ROPES

Lucy goes to Washington! Her student court group has a date to be shown around the nation's capital for an entire weekend by an important politician. But she quickly learns that politicians aren't always that easy to get hold of. In the meantime, Simon wants to be an entrepreneur, so he decides to baby-sit for one of Ruthie's friends. But once Ruthie finds out Simon's plans, it seems Simon will have one more unexpected kid to look after. . . .

DON'T MISS THIS BRAND-NEW, ORIGINAL 7ᵀᴴ HEAVEN STORY

Now Available!

DRIVE YOU CRAZY

Road trip! Mary and Lucy are thrilled their parents are allowing them to drive to Arizona to visit Grandpa Charles and Ginger. Freedom at last, they think, until the car is almost stolen. Unexpected help comes from a runaway teenage girl, whose situation leaves the Camden sisters wanting to help. But how do you help someone who doesn't want it?

Mary Camden had a good reason to be upset.

It was Christmas Eve and, unlike the rest of her family, she wasn't in Glenoak. Nor was she curled up in a warm bed or roasting chestnuts on an open fire. Mary was stranded in the Chicago airport. Alone. Waiting in an endless line of angry travelers. Just her luck.

She took a deep breath and looked out the giant windows of the airline terminal. When her flight from Buffalo had landed, the snow was light, but now a massive blizzard swirled so thick that even the blinking red lights of the runway had been erased from view. All flights were now canceled— including her connecting flight to Los Angeles. Was there any way to get home on a night like this?

She turned to a frustrated man behind her, whose tie had been loosened and retightened so many times it looked like a dirty, crinkled napkin.

"Don't these planes have computers that control their landings?" Mary asked. "They don't need to see the runway, do they?"

The man guffawed. "Computers? Who needs computers? If they had real pilots—fighter pilots—instead of these wimpy civilians in fake corporate uniforms, we'd be home by now."

Mary laughed at the man's feisty attitude. Then she looked at her watch. Her eyes widened. She'd been standing in line for an hour! And not a single airline employee had offered their assistance, or even apologized.

The man grabbed his tie and wiped a streak of doughnut filling from his chin. "What they deserve is a good lawsuit," he barked, loud enough for the attendant to hear. But the attendant was preoccupied with an angry customer—a screaming woman in a fur coat.

Mary sighed, then tried to calm herself down. Maybe she was overreacting. Maybe the situation really was out of the airline's control. . . . But she couldn't deny her irritation. There weren't even enough chairs in the waiting area for the people who'd been stranded there.

The man seemed to be reading her thoughts. "All these people are driving me crazy. Too many of them in too small a space."

Mary's eyes combed the terminal. "There's barely room to stand, let alone to sit. . . ."

The man snorted. "Well, we aren't leaving for a long time. Might as well get comfortable on the cold, dingy floor." He picked up his briefcase. "In fact, I think that's exactly what I'm going to do." And with that, he left the line.

But Mary wasn't giving up so easily. She crossed her arms and considered her options. She could continue to stand in line—knowing it would take hours to accomplish anything—or she could act.

She picked up her bag and charged straight through the line of people.

"Hey, no cutting," a man yelled.

Mary ignored him and stormed up to the check-in desk, where the fur-coated woman was flailing her hands in anger.

"Excuse me!" the woman shouted at Mary. Her fingers were covered with tacky, oversized diamonds.

But Mary was undeterred. She plopped her elbows on the desk and leaned over toward the attendant. "If I were the President of the United States and I demanded to be put on a flight tonight, would you put me on it?"

The attendant, unamused, calmly remarked, "I could put you on a plane, but it still couldn't take off."

The haughty woman tried to look down her nose at Mary, then realized that Mary was taller than she thought. "I am the wife of the governor of California. Do you really think this man would put on a plane before taking care of me?"

Mary ignored the tone in the woman's voice, although she couldn't deny the sinking feeling in the pit of her stomach. If this wealthy, important woman couldn't get on a flight tonight, how could Mary?

Mary looked at the attendant.

"Then can you put me in a hotel?"

"They're all full," the governor's wife cooed, savoring Mary's reaction. "Luckily, there's a suite reserved for me regardless of what city I'm in."

Mary couldn't help firing the woman a venomous look before turning to go. She'd find a hotel room if it was the last thing she did.

Thirty minutes later, Mary had called every hotel in the Yellow Pages except one. She crossed her fingers as she dialed the number. A male clerk picked up the line.

"Don't hang up until you've heard me out!" she began. "Do you have any rooms?"

The clerk sighed, "Sorry—"

Before he could hang up, Mary jumped in. "Even an empty office or a janitor's closet?"

"Sorry, miss. No vacancy."

The line went dead and Mary stood staring at the phone in her hand.

Suddenly, Mary couldn't help but laugh at the irony of her name.

But the laugh quickly turned into a smirk: the name was about the only thing she had in common with her biblical namesake. The Virgin Mary was divine, but Mary Camden . . . What had she ever accomplished besides jail time and a family ousting? The last good thing she had done was win a stupid basketball game—and then trash the gym she'd won it in.

Mary felt really low. She picked up the phone and dialed, hoping Robbie would answer and make her feel better.

The familiar voice of Mary's on-again, off-again boyfriend came through the line. "Hello?"

Mary felt tears welling up in her eyes. "I'm stuck in the stupid Chicago airport. I won't be home for Christmas Eve."

There was a short pause. "Well, you'll be home tomorrow, right? You'll be home for Christmas?"

Mary looked out the window, where the blizzard was raging even more fiercely than before. "I don't know. . . ."

There was another pause, and then Robbie did the very dumbest thing he could have done: he laughed. "Hey, the twins are sick anyway. Maybe I'll get their stomach flu and you'll be the lucky one who misses out."

Mary couldn't believe he was making

light of the situation. "Lucky? You call this lucky?"

"I didn't say you were lucky. I said maybe you'll be the lucky one who misses out. I was trying to make a joke—"

"Well, it's not funny, Robbie! I'm stuck in this stupid place with stupid strangers with no beds and no blankets and no showers!"

"I'm sorry. I wanted to make you laugh. . . ."

Mary wiped away a tear. Lately, it felt like Robbie didn't care about seeing her nearly as much as she cared about seeing him.

"You don't even care if I get home, do you?"

Robbie sighed. "I was trying to make you feel better, that's all, Mary. And it didn't work. So maybe what you need to do is just accept the situation—that's the only thing that will make the night bearable."

That's when Mary felt a tug on her coat. Annoyed, she turned around to find a six-year-old girl staring up at her.

"Where's the bathroom?" the little girl asked.

Mary covered the mouthpiece of the

phone and leaned down. "You see that blue sign way down there, across the hall? That's the girls' bathroom."

The little girl smiled and darted off.

"Hey!" Mary called. "Wait!"

But it was too late. The little girl was already lost in the crowd.

Robbie continued to talk, but Mary found herself missing every other word. That little girl . . . why was she asking about a bathroom? Where were her parents? Her guardians? Who would leave a kid alone in an airport?

"I gotta go!" Mary suddenly exclaimed to Robbie.

She hung up the phone and dashed off after the little girl.